One-Bullet Dilemma

A light sci-fi psychological drama

Joe Benet

A Couple of Writers

This is my first published work, but not my first submitted. While the journey is long, it is also full of wonderful people who donated their time and honesty to improve my writing. So, thank you to my wonderful wife who read my stuff even though it's not her favorite genre, and who put up with listening to multiple "premises without a plot yet." Also, sincere thanks to Sheila for your constant encouragement and feedback. Thanks to Eric for introducing me to "drama without action," and to my dear sister Britta. Finally, to all the others who read and critiqued, you are unnamed here for brevity, but certainly not unappreciated. All of you helped make this novella happen.

CONTENTS

1

Vee Day

NEITHER JOKES, DREAMS, NOR fears of alien first contact ever materialized in Technical Sergeant Lewis Jabril's four years at his post. Each night at this nondescript US Space Force substation, nestled outside an unremarkable North Carolina mountain town, excited him as little as the previous night. It was just a job. Reds, yellows, and oranges of surrounding peaks morphed into blobs of black by the start of each shift. Crisp air tamped down all pleasant scents, leaving a blankness in his nose. Still, before entering the control room, he slapped the overhead banner that read 'Always the Predator, Never the Prey.' His chestnut hand stood out against the white lettering.

"Evening, Sergeant." Specialist Damian Tieg, the only other soldier on duty, greeted Lewis from his desk, sipping coffee from a white mug splattered with a green cartoon alien behind the words, 'Enjoy the probing.'

Eight monitors, each sixty-one-inch diagonal, lined one wall, tracking known assets in this post's sector of space. Servers tucked under a dozen unmanned desks heated the lonely room to toasty temps while they processed raw data from patrolling satellites. The amount of gear echoed the tales of when this post was valuable to the Pentagon. These days, not even the day shifts filled half the seats.

Tieg wiped his mouth. "Second Shift reports nothing unusual. Transition of responsibilities complete. Continuing to monitor five-by-five. It's just you and me, Sarge, and of course the invisible, telepathic, scantily clad female ambassadors from Illumina Five still trying to recruit me as their spy. They say hi."

"Let the good times roll, Tieg. I'll swap server hard drives. You keep eyes on the skies and your rocket in your pocket, please."

No sooner had Lewis turned toward the main server room than warning beeps snagged his ear and reeled him back. An orbiting sentinel reported an anomaly, either a new asset detected or a known one out of place.

Excitement. The evening improved. His predator mode activated. Nightly routines and time-killing distractions faded from the top of his mind, replaced by rusty response protocols and forgotten focus. He planted his feet, straightened his back, drew deliberate breaths, and waited for the initial report.

Tieg swigged his brew, slapped down the mug, and lip-smacked an "ahh" as he rolled two desks down. He scanned readings on two desktop monitors. "It's massive, whatever it is. Bigger than ISS. Not space junk or a comms relay, that's for sure. Starting verification protocols."

Larger than the International Space Station? Three minutes later, a second wave of identical beeps haunted the room.

"Uh, Sarge? That's a separate network. They don't share components. So, either we have simultaneous failures, or two unidentified aerial phenomena emerged in high orbit."

Adrenaline, that long forgotten friend, reintroduced itself to Lewis, like during that first suborbital training flight years ago. As far as he was concerned, space was best experienced from the ground. "Alert SpOC. Classify UAP as prelim but highly suspicious. I'm ordering first shift back and—"

The hot phone, direct link to Space Operations Command, SpOC, read Lewis' mind and preempted Tieg's call, flashing that ominous red and clanging those impatient tones.

"Yessir. This is Technical Sergeant Jabril in command of Cherokee Station … Confirm another station's signal? Yessir, but we scanned two of our own, sector two-one-two and sector two-two-seven."

Lewis snapped fingers at Tieg, snatched a Post-it, and scribbled additional coordinates. "Yessir. Five minutes to confirm."

Some five minutes fly by faster than others. All three contacts looked legit, and more reports rolled in. Whoever, or whatever, hovered in the skies had arrived in force. Lewis paced and mentally cycled through the response protocols, ready to pounce when the next orders arrived.

"So, Sarge, who's the predator here?"

"Always us, Tieg. Never forget that."

2

SHOCKING INTRO

MARK DESPISED WAKING UP in new surroundings and knew immediately this one was bad. A different consistency of night enveloped him: stale, unfamiliar, and uncomfortable. Traveling for work had perks, but that new-bed sensation wasn't one of them. As far as he recalled, he should have been at home in Charlotte, North Carolina, comfy under his own cotton sheets, but this was not his chamber. Unease awoke in him as he awoke in this strange bed. Though he tried to focus on a soothing mantra to remain calm, no lyrics about overcoming fear came to his mind, just an ominous chant sounded out by his thumping heart. *Not – good ... Not – good.*

Open-eyed, only blackness greeted him. *Wow, is that dark.* Coin toss on whether this was a coffin. He lost the flip and sighed relief when he moved aside the sheets and wearily swung his legs over the side of an actual bed. He groaned. A twenty-four-year-old should not feel this sore, ever, not after a simple job interview with alien occupiers for an entry-level marketing role. Only six months since Vee Day and governments already created embassies for the visitors, embassies that needed pamphlets and public communications. No memories surfaced between the moment he walked out of that building and now. *Does this mean I didn't get the job?*

Clunk. The moment his bare feet hit the mausoleum-cold floor, a sound like a large circuit breaker announced a radiant light from a faraway ceiling, illuminating one meter around him while a wall of gloom swallowed the rest of the room. He sat alone in the one-and-only spotlight on an unknown stage thinking he'd rather work behind the scenes.

From black hole dark to supernova bright, Mark's arm instinctively shaded his eyes while they adjusted. This beam could have tanned his pasty white skin. "Hello?" No reply, not even an echo.

A small nightstand against the wall held a bulb-less lamp, useless, but the substitute sun glinted off another chunk of metal next to it: a shiny, large-caliber, semi-automatic handgun. He picked it up, flipped it over and back, the heft filling his palm. He examined it, reading meaningless numbers etched into the side and pressing a button until the magazine released. A single round topped the otherwise empty stack, and none was chambered.

"One bullet? That's not helpful." Still, he replaced the magazine. It fell out and onto the floor. For his second attempt, he slapped it a few times until it held before slipping the tool under his belt, unracked. Cringy online videos had taught him that safety tip, and shooting himself in the leg was last on his to-do list. He'd never hear the end of it from his older brothers. Jocks. Mark had never excelled in sports or much of anything except speaking before thinking and then keeping his head down while walking in the shadow of the crowd.

A stale aroma invaded his nose; musty, earthy, damp. Mark rose, legs wobbly, kept one hand connected to the wall—natural stone, cold and uncaring—and explored his perimeter with the other arm gingerly scouting the dark ahead.

Fingers slid along the cement-gray as smooth and chilly as the ground under his feet. With each shuffle, his spotlight followed as if watching and waiting for his inevitable mistake. The secretive black veil retreated in front but advanced behind, leaving the same single circle of light that now revealed no pictures, no windows, no closets.

Clunk. Clunk. Two more spotlights appeared ten meters away and ten meters apart. Each narrow shaft illuminated an occupied bed while still nothing except night separated the three people. Thank God he wasn't alone.

"Hey, who's there?" Both arms feeling in front, Mark fumbled his way toward someone still covered by bedsheets. Soon, the cusp of his spot found floor-to-ceiling prison bars separating him from the others. He grabbed the metal to test its resolve.

Zap!

<hr>

"Eek!" Willa's high-pitched, feminine voice resounded as white sparks blew some guy away from metal bars, launching him from a single beam of light back into the abyss. That was one hell of a wake-up call. A spotlight scanned the area, weaving back and forth until landing on the sprawled body.

"Hey, are you okay?" Though she had no clue where she was, the guy clearly needed help. She and Dad had spent enough time in the woods, seen enough injuries, that she knew time mattered. She threw aside the sheets and leaped from her bed, but stumbled on stiff, slender legs. "Ow."

The two individual spotlights disappeared, hers and his, replaced by gentle lights that cleared the shadows. Not much blocked her path—single bed behind and small desk and chair to her side.

Barefoot, she wobbled across a sparse, refreshing floor to the prison bars separating her from the unconscious guy, warming her still-awakening stiff muscles like an early morning lumber after sleeping under the stars.

"Don't touch them. They're electrified."

She reared from the nearby voice of the surprise stranger, fists ready, feet spread shoulder width apart, one behind the other, burning sore legs slightly bent but ready to strike. Nobody jumps a rez girl and walks away unhurt. "Who are you? Where am I?"

The man—mid-thirties, olive-skinned, short-but-full beard, dressed in khakis and a business casual, button-down shirt—stood in another cell eyeing his surroundings. The fence between them stretched from the floor to an unseen ceiling. Shadows floated a little higher than a grizzly on his hind legs reaching for food.

The man clutched a handgun.

⌁

"Welcome back, pretty boy."

The light dragged Mark out of his best sleep ever—gentle, soothing. Soon, though, that light turned harsh; bright, blinding, cutting deeper into his throbbing head with each blink. Oh, and that bruised back hurt like a bad day on the backyard football field with older brothers—what a horrible awakening. His hands fished around, sweeping across rough concrete. "What? Is it Taco

Tuesday?" He still wasn't fully awake and resisted the process, longing instead for that pain-free slumber.

"Huh?" A single woman—late-twenties, dressed in a Virginia Woolf t-shirt—squatted a few meters away on the other side of iron rods.

"Did you say something about tacos?" Mark slowly regained his senses and cautiously raised his back to the bedframe. Untucked sheets and a ratty, thin blanket draped the sides of a single mattress on rusty rails.

"No, you did. You're still delirious. I said 'welcome back.' You blacked out cold for an hour, so don't touch these bars again. They're electrified." The cute girl straightened blue jean legs and paced the charged hedge between them; barefoot, inquisitive, eyeing each pole up and down. She had long, straight hair, the blackest in his memory, a flat, tan face with pronounced cheekbones, and dangling feather earrings adorning her neck.

"Electrified? Oh, I thought I dreamed that."

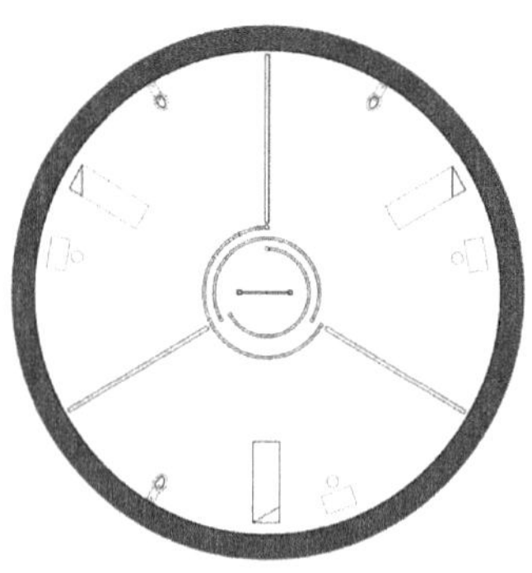

Drawing by Rick Clark

He took a quiet moment to gather his bearings. The space mimicked a decent-sized master bedroom, but sparsely furnished and seemingly hidden in a cave. Two other identical, wedge-shaped rooms, all separated by prison bars with a chest-high metal crossbeam, formed a circle and met in the middle at a small, circular fence, like a pizza with three pieces and the center eaten away. In that center, the fence enclosed a ladder that disappeared into the blackness overhead: presumably the exit. Any ceiling existed higher than the light, taller than a normal room, and the solid walls curved and flowed into the gloom. No clue on where the light originated.

"We have a serious dilemma." A third wheel tramped into the scene, interrupting the couple just getting to know each other. A full beard didn't hide his scowl, and he sported a handgun.

"Whoa, whoa. What's that for?" Mark clambered to his feet, still woozy, only eighty percent sure of his reality.

The newcomer stepped to his metal hedge and strode its length, agitation etched on his face like a tattoo, fist wrapped around the grip but still pointing the weapon to the ground. "Red, how many bullets do you have?"

The lady revealed a surprise from her backside waistband and checked. "Damn, Green. Just one. That's not helpful."

Green, the new guy, aimed his eyes at Mark. "Blue, do you have a gun with a single bullet?"

"Put that away. I'm unarmed." Mark held out both shaky palms.

"Check your bedside."

Mark peered that direction, keeping the hostile barrel in his peripheral, recalled the glint of light from an hour ago, and rolled his eyes. "Yes, yes, now I remember." He reached into his waistband and disclosed an identical weapon. Both cellmates furrowed their brows, as if they'd caught his first fib in a new relationship. "What? I was nearly shocked to death. Give me a moment to remember stuff."

"So what, Green. We each have a gun with one bullet. What's the dilemma?" Red asked.

"Read your new message. It says the last one of us alive goes free."

Mark smirked. "Come on. What does that even mean, last one alive?"

"It means, Blue, that if I want to live, I need a way to kill two strangers with one bullet, and you have the same challenge. The messages from the aliens haven't been wrong yet, and nothing they've done in six months says they joke around." With that, hardened Green, always facing the other two, retreated backwards to his computer—a basic looking home model like Mom used to read emails and print Sudokus, a new revelation for Mark since this was the first he'd seen the room in full light. Green's chair rested with its back to the room in front of a small, cheap, wooden desk; he repositioned it to place the side along the wall. A tankless, lidless toilet sat a couple of meters away.

Mark smirked again because his brain and face would not collaborate on a second expression. "No way. That makes no sense. Why would they do that? They already kill us indiscriminately anytime they want. No, what this means is we need to work together to figure a way out, like an Escape Room. I'll bet there's a lock in each room we'll shoot at exactly the same time. Help me find them."

Mark scrutinized his claustrophobic chamber, hands patting up and down the stone spying for cracks, sensitive cheek feeling for any breeze, ears listening for any sound. Scared heartbeats thumping in his eardrums hindered the search. He spent his next three birthday wishes on finding a clue. The edges of his floor and walls, where bars met stone, were lit blue all around. Red outlined the woman's room; green the guy's. A partial rainbow.

When his investigation looped back to Red, he discovered her standing in place, no longer analyzing her room. Her mouth cracked open as if jaw muscles surrendered to the situation. Eyes, barely blinking, stared at nothing. Her exterior mirrored his internals.

Not knowing what to do next, he faked it and tried to engage her, snap her out of it. "Vibe check. How you feeling?" No response. He needed better marketing. "Hey, don't listen to him. We're all getting out of here alive. I watched you explore your room; you're curious, smart. I want you as my partner, okay? Tell me, where are you from?" Whether the whole *last one alive* bit was true or not, friendly conversation sounded quite soothing at the moment. Work out alliance details later.

A slow headshake scrutinized something he couldn't detect. She shuffled a little and murmured, "Originally, the Pacific Northwest, but I recently began teaching at a university in Lisbon."

"Oh, I love Spain. Flew out of Barcelona once. Is Lisbon nearby?"

Red fixed dead, dreary eyes on him for a moment, criticizing, then shook her head, rolled those eyes, and restarted her search. "Yeah, it's a suburb."

"Oh, wow. I think I visited a park overlooking the ocean. How fun would it be if we hiked right by each other? Do you like to hike? Maybe when we get out, we hit a trail together."

No reply, just a slow, horizontal head bob, like a gentle, autonomous 'no,' that mouth still ajar. He watched for a few moments, hoping she would liven up a notch, say anything to keep the conversation going, show at least a glint of interest, rescue him from rambling. Instead, she continued to scan her tiny environment, but at least seemed more alert than moments ago.

"So, what were you saying earlier? Was that 'pretty boy' as in let's get out of here and have a drink together, or 'pretty boy' as in I should eat more meat and hit the gym? Because I can see it both ways, to be honest."

"Are you being serious right now?" She focused on her inspection and appeared in no mood for distractions.

"No, just getting my mind off my sore back, but let's start simple. What's your name, and where are we?"

"Not sure where we are, but I'm Red; you're Blue, and Green's over there."

Blue waved, but Green never saw. No spot was out of earshot, but that roommate at least was not interested in conversation. "Colors? Blue? No, that's not my name. I'm Mark."

"Welcome to the suck, Mark. Wish the circumstances were, well, anything else. I'm Willa. He's Rasheed, but the messages on our computers address us by our room color. See mine? Red all around, even up the frame of the billets. Colors sort of stuck as our nicknames."

That explained the partial rainbow. "Yeah, computers. Right." Blue strode to his desk and jiggled the mouse. "Let's contact the police, or our families, get some answers." His mood enlivened at his bright idea.

"Can't. We only get inbound info from a very select menu, and the aliens know everything about our life. Everything. They brought us here. I think revealing the info they have is meant as a threat, or maybe not."

Spamming the Enter key proved her point. Nothing on the screen looked like a way out. "Do the messages say *how* we got here? Last thing I remember was answering interview questions about dissonance, you know, for marketing. I was applying for a government public relations role."

"So, a collaborator?"

"No, no. That's harsh. I'm just a guy trying to survive and thrive under the new reality. I'm adaptable." Armed roommates who viewed him as one of the hated occupiers would be bad for his odds of escape.

"Hmm." She never stopped surveying, keen eyes fully resurrected and back on the hunt for clues. "We don't know how we got here either. I was sitting in my bombed-out apartment, writing a story in my mind. Green analyzed stocks, I think, in London, but he lives in Iran. All I know is we didn't get here the easy way. I'm bruised all over."

"Ooo, can I see? I learned a little first aid."

"No, some are on my legs and thighs."

"Okay, so maybe later?" He cringed inside before he finished the sentence. *Maybe later? What kind of response was that, Mark? How dumb.*

"Don't be a creep; this is serious."

Serious indeed, the most surreal moment in his life, but he wouldn't figure out this problem alone, just like he never got his way at dinner discussions while growing up as the youngest in a large family. Nobody joined his side then, and he always lost. He needed a friend, and he definitely needed to live more than he needed that Disney World vacation when every other sibling voted for the beach. Now he may die without ever visiting the Magic Kingdom. A tantrum wouldn't solve this present dilemma either, only cooperation and teamwork. Sure of nothing else, but scared and now embarrassed as well, he stomped as close to the zappy circular fence in the middle as he dared and called out, "Even if Rasheed is right, there's no way to win. Think about it. Whoever shoots first loses. Let's say I shoot Rasheed. Now I'm out of ammo, and Willa kills me. I lose. So, let's just take a breath, work together, and nobody shoot first."

3

T-Bone and a Nuke

L EWIS JABRIL FLUNG HIS car door closed and waited for the right beat in the music thumping in his earbuds, the brief dramatic pause in the song, before pressing the lock button on his remote.

Beep-beep.

A vibrant chill powered the night air while a breeze rustled empty tree branches in a playful dance. The meteorologist looked dour at his latest prediction, but Lewis sang his own cheery tune.

"Let it snow, let it snow, let it snow."

Before entering the control room, he slapped the overhead banner with gusto. Always the Predator, Never the Prey. It didn't matter how positive the press releases read about Earth's new friends. He remained suspicious, and they remained in his theater of operations.

"Evening, Sergeant."

"Tieg. How are you this evening?"

"Just enjoying the probing." Specialist Damian Tieg lifted his favorite coffee mug. "Hey, you know tonight is Vee plus one month? A full thirty days since you and I first reported those bastards in our heavens. What's the Vee for, again? Visitors? Visitation? I can't recall."

"The Vee means its own thing now. The origins are for etymologists to debate." He noted the sarcastically stunned look on his subordinate's face. "Yeah, I know words, but to be fair, I looked it up yesterday."

"Oh, previous shift dumped a problem on us."

"Ooo, a problem, you say?" Lewis rubbed hands together as if warming up. "Nothing like a good space puzzle. Hit me, Tieg."

"Russian Molniya Asset Seventeen, a cold standby comms satellite, pinged for the first time in months. It's off from our projected location, so we get to analyze and suggest an optimization to the algorithms. Tracking now."

"Sounds like a perfect night. We suspect those serve a dual purpose. I'll bet they tinkered with the orbit for a military op. Let me get my coffee."

Fuel in hand and mind already revving, he sat at his workstation next to Tieg and crunched the data.

"Hey, Sarge. Looks like you were right. Orbit is not off; it's completely different. Honestly, it may even be an unknown asset mimicking Seventeen's ID."

"Confirmed. New path is not a minor deviation from previous. Switch from orbital analysis to orbital projection protocols. Get me a refined track while I alert asset owners."

"Uh, Sarge. We have a problem."

"Fortunately, we are adept problem solvers."

"Russian Molniya Asset Seventeen on track to collide with Visitor Asset Eight over central Argentina in one hour. Think they see it?"

"Good question, Tieg. I don't know, but their drooling over our facilities makes me guess not. Maybe they need our tech. Either way, can't assume they see it. Alerting the brass upstairs." He picked up the hot phone to SpOC. "Tech Sergeant Jabril in command of Cherokee Station, reporting possible collision." After scribbling a few notes, he read the data to the Luey on the phone. "Yessir." He hung up. "Orders are to verify, continue tracking, and report any changes."

That's what he and his lone wingman did: watched the alien ship parked in the same spot, picked up the same red handset, recited the same report minus fifteen minutes to impact until no more reports mattered. A Russian satellite, presumably, smashed into a peaceful—also presumably—alien spaceship at high speed. He never learned the full extent of the damage, but watched that ship drop altitude precariously low to the ground before recovering and reentering orbit. Later, online videos showed smoke billowing from the side.

"What does this mean, Sarge?"

"What this means, Tieg, is that our visitors aren't invincible." Lewis leaned back and locked hands behind his head, swiveling in his chair.

"They may be vulnerable, sure, but now are they pissed?"

"Clandestine comms active, Sarge. All hail Illumina Five Spy Master Tieg."

"Stop using your real name, chump. You'll get yourself killed." Lewis, frustrated Space Force vet, knew at least that much about spy craft. "It doesn't matter how encrypted or embedded your data stream, someone's going to read it." All hail documentaries to fill lonely weekends. Maybe, just maybe, those lessons would keep his talkative friend alive.

While the suits upstairs appeared fine with capitulating to ever-escalating demands from the solar newcomers, grunts on the ground, like him and Tieg, grew disillusioned with abductions, executions, and worldwide brownouts. Their ships had flown across a galaxy but needed Earth's resources to keep from *tragically* crashing into a major city? Plus, curious civilians with a camera who merely strolled too close to an ambassador triggered a deadly response that they justified by claiming to feel threatened. Don't understand our tech or our culture? Yeah, right. They learned diplomatic immunity easily enough.

Making those assertions harder to believe, the few alien ambassadors that walked around planet side stood a half-meter taller than most humans, draped head-to-toe in flowing robes of bright colors. Lewis likened them to ancient Chinese royalty. They never revealed their bodies or faces in public. Maybe breathing gear underneath their clothes bulked up their image, but either way, they looked like they could handle themselves in a fistfight.

Rumors floating around now implied the aliens wanted to *improve* society by eliminating certain undesirables. Sickening. And all for what? So far, just three months of undelivered promises of advanced tech and interstellar trade. Time for grunts to do something about it.

"Fine. How about ... Illumina Sex? Because I'm an addition to the Illumina Five family, and I'm so sexy." Tieg squatted in the crawl space under the main server room floor in the dark underbelly of their quiet Space Force outpost. Lights out except for enough blue in each aisle to keep from tripping on the occasional step ladder or strands of cable, air conditioning supplementing the underground chill, the dank basement housed enough server power to crunch readouts from dozens of sensors mounted on dozens of military assets orbiting the occupied skies above.

Lewis squatted beside Tieg. "I'm not calling you Sex. Now, quiet while I record the invite. This is Sarge, broadcasting on invite address one. Tonight's party is in house seven. I repeat, tonight's party is in house seven." Lewis pressed his stop button. "Loop that on channel one, then switch me to seven."

Tieg tapped into the cables sending high-speed encrypted data to their regional processing center. Voice-only packets on top of that torrent should hide well, but as an added measure, his code pushed those spy bits only when the real data slowed or surged one-sigma from the mean. Net effect: no peak packet anomaly triggered by the techs monitoring for problems, nor any of his packets sent by themselves where they stood out on a scope. That drone could be smart when he tried. The spy-without-a-spy-name also watched the facility's cameras for unwanted visitors. This was a private conversation.

"Seven is hot." Tieg pointed the go finger at Lewis.

"This is Sarge. Anyone else here?"

"Italy is on."

"Philippines here."

Space Force global allies checked in, grunts on distant ground.

"Pham is on." Ah, Pham Xuan An, Sarge's favorite coconspirator from Vietnam who grasped his role—and his risk—and picked an appropriate nom de guerre. Agenda item for next time: covert call signs.

Sarge kicked off the meeting. "Clock is ticking, so let's begin while others join. Thank you all for your courage. First topic is local updates—"

Tieg and angry beeps interrupted. "Sarge, a sentinel reports ... a launch." He peered into his wireless tablet. "Indian Asset One just shot a nuke."

The launch triggered every sensor to grab high-resolution data. Italy sputtered on the choked line. "What's going on? Did someone say nuke?"

"We gotta scoot. Brass will call any second. Listen for deets of our next meeting on invite two." Sarge adjourned the underground resistance gathering, then he and Tieg scooped gear and dashed upstairs. Tieg sat at his cubicle stacked with four monitors while Lewis stood at his adjoining station near the hot phone.

"Sitrep," Lewis's voice boomed loud enough to surprise himself. Until Tieg replied, Lewis' elevated heart rate formed a battle song in his ears. Tonight, he had no children of his own to protect, but when he did, he needed their world to be safe.

"A single Badala-II fired three minutes ago from 1600 kilometers above Madagascar, bearing five-zero degrees, zee plus, at 21.6 kilometers-per-hour, on track to strike ... Visitor Asset Four above Sri Lanka in ... eight minutes."

The main wall of monitors already streamed the hot sector. A blinking short line moved northeast over the Indian Ocean toward a solid triangle, faded dashes in front predicting the flight path, counting down the pixels until a nuclear warhead blasts a visiting alien species. At least the first shot wasn't aimed his direction. *The counterpunch, though ...*

The Imperial March, Darth Vader's theme song, blared from the hot phone, Tieg's contribution to ease the boredom of long nights with no action. "This is Sarge, uh, Tech Sergeant Jabril in command of Cherokee Station. Yessir, we confirm a hot flare. Source Indian—"

"Target, I need the target," now blared from the handset. Lewis cringed and moved his ear away until the volume subsided.

"Uh, yessir. Target is Visitor Asset Four. Impact in eight minutes. Please advise." Lewis dropped the phone from his ear and stared. "He hung up."

Tieg kept eyes on the data. "What next, Sarge?"

"Don't call me that here, not anymore."

"Sorry, Sergeant. We supposed to just sit and watch the first hostile nuclear explosion in space, ever? You know that means an EMP, right? India just self-inflicted a massive wound."

"Nah, it's too high. Won't be a problem. As for us, we monitor, track, and report. That's our job, and we do it better than anyone, but this is a predator move, Tieg. Hit them on their home turf, in their blind spot. You gotta respect the swing."

Server lights blinked, unaware of the tension, and dedicated processors crunched numbers, performing their duties like countless civilians trucking goods across the nighttime roads and selling snacks at rest stops.

"Whoa. Visitor Asset Four is zee plus, gaining altitude fast. Need a minute to calculate." Tieg danced his fingers across the keyboard and touchscreens.

"That's evasive maneuvers. That's advanced signals intelligence," Lewis mused. "So, they can't avoid a 1600-kilogram Molniya satellite traveling at 2500 kilometers per hour, but they detect a 35,000-kilogram, 2-meter-wide cylinder going nine times that fast? Sus, but it gives us an idea of their capabilities."

"Or we warned them." Tieg's insight amazed him, and simultaneously frightened him. "Think about it. SpOC calls, just wants the target, and two minutes later, target evades."

He stared at the blinking short line inching ever closer to its prey scrambling in retreat. A slow-speed dodge from a knock-out blow. Regardless of the backroom politics, this was history, and he had not only a front-row seat to the action but also a vested interest in the outcome. What could his enemy do, and how well could they do it? The line filled in more pixels in front.

"Any countermeasures yet?"

"No, just the evasion. It's a footrace to the top. Three minutes to impact."

Two sets of eyes glued to the huge monitor. Lewis gulped. Tieg tapped his foot against the desk.

"Two minutes … One minute. Missile matched target's altitude."

Very few empty pixels remained dark between the blinking line and solid triangle. The final one took an eternity to light up, closing the gap.

"Twenty seconds; altitudes are too close to differentiate. It'll be close."

The line disappeared under the solid triangle. No flash indicated an explosion.

"Zero."

Sarge's breath froze in his throat, solidarity with the collective spirit of dozens of other eyes around the globe watching the same scene. Time to learn history's judgment.

"Miss!" Tieg flung two arms high in victory. Lewis exhaled through pursed lips. Who doesn't celebrate avoiding a nuclear war with a race who may or may not have nukes?

A blinking line peeked from the other side of that solid triangle, growing longer by the minute. A sober realization ended the revelry like flashing police lights outside his last high school party. That nuke, fuel now exhausted but momentum still alive, flung forward after missing its prey—forward and downward. Dashed lines projecting in front widened and spread across a vast area of eastern China. Sensors needed more time to narrow the prediction.

He snatched the hot phone handset from its cradle and readied his delivery. "This is Tech Sergeant Jabril in command of Cherokee Station reporting a falling flare. Yessir. Missile from Indian Asset One missed target Visitor Asset Four and is now in freefall. Projected impact: twelve minutes somewhere in eastern China, southwest of Nanjing, south-by-southeast of Hefei. Sir, the Indians need to send the disarm signal. Yessir. Cherokee Station continuing to monitor five-by-five."

He returned the handset, roller-coaster of emotions flinging through his body. Only training kept him thinking. He stared at Tieg but spoke to no one in particular. "They have to disarm. The Chinese don't have anti-missile capabilities, and ours are too far away."

"Sergeant. This is weird."

Lewis repeatedly glanced at the main monitors after sitting and massaging his computer for more info, eager for Tieg's punchline.

"Visitor Asset Four turned and is chasing the nuke, dropping altitude," Tieg reported. The solid triangle pointed northeast now and moved behind the blinking short line.

"Is it gaining, trying to snatch it out of the sky, or shoot it down?"

"Can't tell. Need more readings." A watched pot never boils, and a watched progress bar never completes. "Ugh, come on already. Got it. Huh, weird."

"What, Tieg? The same weird, or a new weird?"

"Visitor's keeping a steady distance. Not gaining. Not sure why. Watching? Learning? Trash talking because they dodged a bullet? Are we witnessing space rage?"

Lewis kept his fingers typing, his mouse clicking, his CPU humming, rapidly assessing and discarding scenarios.

Oh, no.

"Tieg, switch to SigInt and verify my readings. Parameters in your folder."

"Yessir. Signals Intelligence it is. Please hold. Our crack staff is processing your request." Tieg rolled his chair to the monitor on his far right and silently read, typed, pointed to his screen, and finally leaned back. "So, if I understand your theory correctly, first, our Thai ground-based listening post picked up electromagnetic frequencies we suspect originated with the alien ship. Second, it is a narrow beam aimed toward the falling flare—based on not seeing the same spike in Bangladesh and Ho Chi Minh City. Third, those frequencies encompass what we suspect India uses to disarm its space-based nukes. If those conditions hold, conclusion, Visitor Asset Four is either attempting to disarm the missile or block India from doing so. Most likely the latter since they don't know the codes."

"Yep." He waited, watched Tieg stare back, wondered what he thought.

"Signal strength on the ground is stronger than any asset we track pumps out, but then again, they all run on batteries. Who knows what powers alien ships these days?"

"I certainly don't, but if it powers interstellar travel, it can power a clearer radio station."

"We'd need the boys from NASA to rule out natural phenomena."

"Sure, but anything from deep space hits a wider area on Earth than this."

"No clue. I watch soccer on the weekends, not science shows," Tieg admitted.

Lewis glanced at the countdown on his screen. Four minutes to impact. Four minutes until he knew if his planet's newest sightseers could disarm a nuclear arsenal or could callously fly to a better viewing spot and watch it explode while sipping beers and eating chicken tenders. Just another cheesy action movie night for them.

Tieg continued the war gaming with an accusation. "What if India doesn't want to disarm?"

Lewis digested the inference and played defense counsel. "Start a nuclear war with China? Tensions are not that high."

"No, but maybe India views it as a win-win. Hit the aliens, gain huge cred on the world stage as bold leaders, or hit China and, meh, who cares? That's why they launched from the asset they did when they did."

"Note to self: do not tick off Damian Tieg. He's a cunning so-and-so."

"Well, that's just good life advice, Sergeant. Three minutes. Maybe India doesn't want to disarm, gave visitors the wrong codes, so now it looks like the aliens shot the missile and guided it toward China."

Ugh. Too many options.

"Two minutes. Hey, Sergeant," Tieg murmured, soft and serious, not quite a whisper but more like a personal pledge.

"Yeah?"

"How about ... Illumina Five-by-Five?"

"Drop the Illumina. Everyone knows your fetish, but yeah, Five-by-Five is perfect."

Two sets of warrior's eyes connected. Years of training for the worst, hoping for the best, nightmares of war, daydreams of peace, culminated in this moment of fate, out of their hands but within their sight.

"One minute. Hey, Sergeant."

"Yeah."

"How will they retaliate? Will they differentiate India from the rest of us?"

"Specialist Damian Tieg, that is one fantastic question." Sarge contemplated deeply those terminating seconds, and long after the flash in eastern China blazed on monitors across the world.

4

Ready Player One

"There's our target—Gang Fan. A bit of a wild one, so take your time and make that taser shot clean. I don't want a fist fight tonight." Squad Leader swiped the details onto the screen hung inside the dark van: Gang's photo, brief bio, and current location working the night shift on a high-rise construction site. A slight bump in the road jiggled the words as the van weaved its way through the Ho Chi Minh City streets.

"Any idea why they want this guy?"

"No clue. New bosses with the giant orbital cannons hand me a profile and tell me to deliver a candidate to this secure facility before the end of the week. A little bruising doesn't matter as long as he's alive and functioning. I don't ask, and maybe I don't end up there myself."

Only Vee plus six months and already humans had turned on each other to do the aliens' dirty work. The transport parked along the boundary of the employee lot and waited for mealtime.

"There's Mr. Fan. Good, he's heading to his car to eat alone, as usual. This mungen loser has no family, no friends, nobody to miss him, and therefore nobody to report him missing. Gear up."

The abduction team donned black masks to complete their dark ensemble and readied batons. Starting with lights out and a gentle roll, their vehicle crept along the asphalt from behind their unaware prey until that delicate sound aroused his curiosity.

"He made us. Go, go, go!"

Tires screeching twice the final several meters, the van first burned rubber to close the distance then squealed to a stop, side door slamming open while still rolling, point man leaping, squatting, and lining up the knock-out shot.

Gang chucked his hardhat, deflecting the aim. Only one prong from the taser hit.

The follow-up guy emerged.

Gang, out of helmets, loaded a screwdriver from his tool belt and flung it hard, followed by a wrench, hammer, tape measure, and level. Left and right hands alternated the barrage.

Two squad mates ducked and dodged their way closer, flanking the feisty carpenter, until one took another crack at the takedown. Clean shot. Two prongs from his taser punctured the denim around Gang's legs.

The shocked one stiffened, convulsed, and fell to the ground.

Three other squad mates joined. Each grabbed a limb and flung the limp body into the abyss, bangs from him bouncing against the far van wall echoing from inside. They escaped into the dark. Mission accomplished, and another payday.

"Strip him."

As the transit shadowed the sparse nighttime traffic, drawing no undue attention, the gang prepped the body with a procedure Squad Leader didn't care to understand. A series of hyposprays injected who knows what into Gang's legs, thighs, and across the body; each powerful *pfft* pumped vials of red, green, and blue, some into blood, others into muscles. Nothing but bruises remained to confirm the process.

"What're those for?" one member asked Squad Leader.

"No clue. Something about neuro-stimulators and holograms. Side effects, though, include short-term memory loss. So even if he saw our faces, he wouldn't remember."

Once at the secure facility—an empty lot used as a playfield in a residential neighborhood—the squad lowered Gang's body on a rope down a twenty-meter deep, underground ladder encircled by a fence, not much concern as he bumped the rungs along the descent.

Up top, Squad Leader's earpiece crackled as he stood watch, ready to shoo away any wandering insomniac. *"Boss, which cell?"*

"Let me check. I always confuse the colors." He pulled up the file. "Blue. Put him in the blue cage. No, no clue what that means."

5

Chew on That

B LUE SAT AT HIS computer screen, excited to chat with his brother for the first time in a while—since before the invasion six months ago—stoked someone else in the world still lived outside of this dank chamber. He wasn't sure how he earned access to this audio-only lifeline, nor did he care. He just wanted to hear a friendly voice, and he craved information. A clue on what to do would help, too. The past four days had dragged with hours of intense debates and philosophical scenarios, interspersed with silent reflection—oh, and free food that miraculously appeared when he wasn't looking. Pizza was his favorite.

"You know the backstory as well as I do, Mark. They came out of nowhere, showed up everywhere, and took over half the planet just by nuking a single city. Some of us fight, some supposedly win, but mostly our leaders negotiate, which means submitting to alien rule regardless of the price. This is where you come into the story. What you don't know is there are dozens of these rooms around the world. We get to watch in real time while you determine our fate. I hate to break it to you, but you are entertainment for our new overlords. They love watching you squirm. More importantly, though, you are like sinister dice.

You represent pre-determined demographics, and when one of you dies in that room, a percent of those people is culled from the herd—all your demographics, and all government sanctioned."

"What do you mean 'all' my demographics?"

"Starts with your city. You die, a chunk of your city dies. Then a smaller portion of your state and a few from your country, but that's not all. You're twenty-four, so you now represent twenty- to twenty-eight-year-olds. Plus, everyone in your room has a similar health index, so no matter what happens, a small percent of eighty to eighty-sixes ... dead, which is sad, right? Because they're all so young and fit. Don't worry about me; I'm a fifty-five."

"My health matters?"

"Yep, and your faith."

"Wait, I represent an entire faith? I don't even know for sure what I believe, especially now. How did they label me?"

"I don't know. Probably an algorithm."

Red's conversation spilled into the entire chamber. "What the hell? Druids are a real thing?"

Blue's brother continued. "Oh yeah, they bucketed Miss 'two-way traffic' over there with a hodgepodge of all the world's religions based on 'respect or worship of nature.' No, it doesn't make sense. That's just what the game stats tell us. Keep an eye on her. She's tougher than she looks. Grew up on a rez, one of the few to go to college."

"Does our race matter?"

"Nope. Apparently, we're all the same; simply conflicted humans who can't get our act together. Hey, timer's about to expire. Listen to me ..." Here comes the lecture. "Forget demographics; forget stats. Nothing you do in that room hurts this family except getting yourself killed, so don't do that. I still owe you a holiday headlock. And don't you dare lose your faith over this. You're not a fighter, Mark, but you are the smartest guy I know, and you care about people. Now is not the time to whine about not getting your way like when we were kids. Now is the time to step up and figure it out."

Blue's screen faded to black, and with it his enthusiasm. No clue on next steps, and no partner to help. His brother possessed more confidence than brains. Still, Blue agreed with the advice. He needed a plan.

Plan your work, then work your plan. Whoever thought up that slogan led a boring life, Blue mused. Where's the room for inspiration, for creativity? To be fair, though, it dawned on him that all his life he never solved a problem solo—siblings growing up, other college students on class projects, and a creative team at marketing firms. On his own, in this cave, ideas failed to flow and quickly dried up in the clammy air.

He feared that today's thought may be his last, so he forced his full concentration on sitting and staring at the spot on his desk where food magically appeared every day. If aliens can get food in, maybe three innocent prisoners could get out. If he only solved one problem in his brief life, this one would do.

"Psst." One of his cellmates tried to get his attention. He shooed them away and remained focused on the bare spot.

"Psssst. Hey, whatcha doing? I'm bored and Green's sleeping." Red's whisper floated across the room.

He glanced at her, back to the still-empty space, over to sleeping Green, then back to his desk. He kept his eyes trained there while rising and tiptoeing backwards toward her, eyes flitting often to avoid a repeat of *The Shocking Intro*—his roommates' name for his painful discovery of the electrified bars. That embarrassing story will probably outlive him.

Once close enough, he whispered back. "I'm working on a plan to escape."

"Yeah, what plan? Staring your desk into submission, so it helps us?"

He furrowed his brow, momentarily breaking his gaze to question her while she grinned. "Huh? No. I'm trying to figure out how our food shows up. Aliens fly shuttles to the ground, so I doubt they have teleport tech."

"How's that help?"

"Not sure, but I figure any way to get food in means a way for us to leave."

"Smart. Any luck?"

"No. Not yet. Want to help?"

"Nah, I'm good."

Blue glared at her. "What, you have a better idea? I'm all ears if you do."

"Hey, keep it down. Green's sleeping, jeez. I just meant you had it covered, and I'm not very observant. Sorry." She backed away, palms forward, gesturing for him to do the same.

He gazed again at his desktop, incredulous to find the very spot that mere moments ago was barren now held the day's meal tray.

"No." He quick-stepped to it, scanning all around for residual clues—up, down, seam between floor and wall. Nothing. He slammed both palms flat onto the desk and hung his head in defeat. The scent of lemon-grilled chicken breast and roasted carrots did not comfort him.

Turning his neck, he glimpsed Red already eating, raising her plastic fork in a food toast as if to say, "Good luck with that idea." Maybe she had distracted him on purpose.

Working his plan was harder than planning his work, and now meant waiting for another full day.

Lewis chucked his cards on the kitchen table.

"Fold, even though I know you're bluffing."

Tieg, his only guest, smirked while raking his winnings. "Next time you'll have to call and find out."

"Just deal and turn up the volume. I can't hear what Blue's saying."

Tieg replied while reaching for the remote. "He's not talking, only staring at his desk, trying to figure out where their food comes from. Did it yesterday, too, but Red distracted him from his goal as fine ladies do."

"Huh. Never thought about it, but where does their food come from? I just see them eating."

Tieg scrunched his nose. "Don't know. Want to bet a blue chip on it?"

"You're on. I say they beam it in."

"Oo, I was gonna go with that. Okay, in that case, I'll say the aliens drug them and wheel it right in like room service."

"Seriously? Have you seen that already, and you're scamming me?"

"No, swear it. I have no clue."

The two gamblers stared at the screen while taking turns cutting the deck and passing a white chip to the high card. Blue maintained his vigil.

Soon, Lewis noticed movement. "Oo, switch to Blue's wide angle." Tieg clicked that camera's thumbnail, promoting it to full screen. The top of the frame ended at the border between light below and darkness above—nobody knew what, exactly, hovered overhead. A drone drifted down from that darkness carrying a food tray. It landed it on the desk right next to an unmoving Blue, unhooked, and returned to the void.

"What the ...? Blue never noticed. How is that possible?" Lewis rubbed the back of his head. "Click on Red's wide-angle and rewind thirty seconds."

Tieg complied, and the two watched as she lay awake on her bed, staring right at her delivery drone. She never stirred until Blue yelled "No way" when he found his food right next to his elbow.

Tieg stared at Lewis, mouth agape. "That's weird, but pay up." He held out his hand. "They didn't beam it in."

He slapped Tieg's hand away. "They didn't drug them either, chump, but I agree. That is quite the weirdness."

6

Hit Them Where It Helps

"**N**O COMMENT? CAN YOU believe these jokers?" Lewis, aka 'Sarge,' spewed indignation into an empty room, cloistered in his bedroom lit by a single computer screen but joined online by his growing group of resistance. "A nuke takes out a rural Chinese village, and after a month, our visitors still have nothing to say."

"That's whack, for sure, yet shows more cojones than our politicians these days. Welcome to Vee plus four months." Tieg, aka Five-by-Five, added the color commentary from his own undisclosed location. His code enabled the two to take these meetings remote but still piggyback on Space Force pipelines with IP addresses spoofed from the Department of Education. According to Tieg, their IT team couldn't spell 'IP address' so would be less likely to trace them, and they just *loved* watching the public feeds from various space stations. So, this shadow conversation should blend right in.

Italy—the femme fatale deceptively codenamed Donnaiolo—chimed in. "Smart, actually. If you blame them, you now think they have nukes, though we can't confirm that. So, they look more powerful."

Philippines—Miong—took the baton. "Or, piece together the trajectory, the radiation signature, and leaked Indian space radar readings, and you might conclude that the aliens tried to stop the nuke. Now they're our friends."

"Though we all know they jammed the signal, preventing India from disarming it mid-flight. Almost childlike, if you think about it. Like they threw a tantrum. 'Nuke me? Pfft, nuke you!'" The calm Vietnamese Pham Xuan An, no real name ever shared, sighed into his mic.

"Yup, and India can't claim the launch without bearing the responsibility. Win-win-win for the visiting team. Divide us two ways and come out ahead three times, thanks to the fog of war. Doesn't help that Space Force won't release their data," Sarge commiserated. "Which reminds me, any intel on that mishap with the Russian satellite?"

Nobody contributed new info, just the same possibilities. Perhaps someone spoofed the ping to hide their true identity and wanted to test alien defenses. Or, the Russians really lost track of it, our algorithms need tweaking, and it was just an accident. No matter the truth, the solar newcomers milked it—and flew more concessions back to orbit. The latest rumor listed free cleaning supplies and several janitors—itemized as 'native talent supply.'

"Let's talk tactics. Where do our strengths match up to their weaknesses?" Chairman Sarge moved to the next agenda item. "How can we hit them?"

Donnaiolo pointed out that it didn't matter why the Russian space junk hit the ship. The fact that it caused damage counted. The aliens couldn't detect and evade all debris thrown at them, and she advocated for hacking and coordinating missile attacks. She preferred space launches since they were harder to spot.

"Aliens evaded the Indian nuke." Miong stirred the conversational wok.

Dang, now Sarge's stomach grumbled.

Thirty minutes ticked by with spicy debates about collaborators at the highest levels tipping off the visitors who occupied more of the human psyche each day.

"Maybe." Pham wound down the bickering, then captivated the covert channel with his insights. "But even if someone backdoor'd a warning, the alternative was allowing a preemptive, hostile strike against a species whose existence alone advances human understanding by centuries, and, need I remind you, who never attacked us. At the time, we couldn't justify war. If you want to understand our tactical situation, think about the British Empire in the Polynesian islands. A warship floats off your shoreline, a ship larger than your village's biggest building. No matter how high you aim or how hard you throw, your arrows and spears can't touch it, and once they know approximately where your village sits, they can pound it with shells, all day and all night. Sure, you can row a boat out to fight, but you're sunk before you leave the shore. Sure, you can resist from the jungle, hoping they never sight your cooking fires, but as long as they can float, they can kill."

"We don't know that they have artillery. Grainy footage we have of their ships suggests more of a transport shape, not a warship." Five-by-Five posted the pics on the channel.

Pham digested the thought for a quiet moment before replying. "Perhaps, or they transported orbital guns? Besides, British shells weren't that accurate or deadly compared to explosives today and still did the job. All the aliens have to do is quick-trip to an asteroid belt, gather giant rocks in their cargo hold, and push them out the airlock from orbit. They'll be slow compared to a real asteroid, yet big enough still means powerful. They'd hurt us bad."

"The Indians aimed high and threw hard enough to hit them back. Visitors got lucky they had a collaborator on the payroll," Donnaiolo suggested.

"True. Theoretically, those half-naked Polynesian soldiers could have built palm-tree trebuchets on top of their mountains and thrown lava rocks, sunk the best in the royal fleet, but they didn't know how. We hold more advantages than an islander, yet still don't know how to reach them up there. We don't have X-Wing fighters. The point remains. Space is our enemy's strength."

"So, we hit them on the ground, on our home turf." Sarge steered the topic toward solutions. "What does that look like?"

"Find their collaborators." Five-by-Five threw out the first idea.

"Kill their ambassadors," Miong wasn't holding back.

"Hit their One-Bullet Dilemma rooms." Pham's comment silenced the channel. "Visitors hold a stronger tactical advantage than their ships floating out of reach off our shores. They are masters of psychological manipulation. In four short months, they've played our fears and desires, convinced half our governments to send free resources, arrest protestors, pardon killings, with nothing but empty promises in return. Now we've confirmed the rumors from three independent sources—they've duped those same leaders to sanction mass killings to reduce our population. Who knows what logic they used? All we know is that in two months we'll start livestreaming humans pitted against each other in some sick game to determine the fate of millions. No bullet-shaped nukes, just rocket-shaped bullets aimed at each other. We'll defeat ourselves before the visitors fire a single shot."

There was no silence like digital silence.

Pham brought it home. "Let's turn their strength against them. It's happening on our turf, so within our reach. It's removing their strength, psychology, and turning it into ours: resolute resistance recruits."

"You thought this through, Pham. I like it." Sarge seconded the motion. "The idea of OBDs, One-Bullet Dilemma rooms, will disgust plenty of people, but they will feel powerless to act. We'll give them that power." His teenage protestor years flashed across his mind, this time with grown-up stakes. "It's your idea, Pham, so you run that department."

A unanimous vote set course and sealed fates. Sarge leaned back in his rolling chair, satisfied with the progress, comfortable now that the group made a plan. "We'll need a follow-up, an offensive ground game for when we recruit enough."

In the waning minutes, the nascent resistance movement leaders finalized the broad strokes. Donnaiolo would plan an attack from space-based assets, maybe even high-altitude fighter jets. Miong would track down and either turn or eliminate collaborators. Five-by-Five would disseminate intel and keep the group's encryption fresh. Sarge would run overall coordination and vet new recruits. All were to keep an ear to the ground for targets of opportunity.

"Congratulations, everyone. We are now either patriots or traitors. Meeting adjourned."

7

Fuel, Not Fear

"**Y**OU DO NOT LOOK so good, my friend." Russian Grigory expressed matter-of-fact indifference, not genuine concern. What could he do, really, standing alone in a separate prison cell locked in some windowless, old Soviet style cinder block structure? This was what life dealt him, and this he would fight like any and all who threatened him. Fight and survive. Try to push him out of business, he'll push your brother over a second-story balcony. At least this time he had a handgun.

The third and final cellmate, Bara from Czechoslovakia, joined the careless encouragement from his adjoining room. "Yeah, Tanek, stop trying to climb out. You should relax. We were enjoying your company." All three respected the electricity surging through the bars separating them from the central ladder.

Calm Grigory desired escape, but Tanek scrapped for it. He sweat profusely while scratching bricks, clinging to and clawing at grout lines, trying to reach the ceiling hidden by a thick, gray smoke shield that blended into the dismal walls. In between hops with hands extended high, he massaged his left arm, alternating that hand between clenched fist and extended fingers.

Exhausted, Tanek finally relaxed and hunched over, side against the wall, palms on knees, heaves fading into huffs. He waved off Grigory's concerns but spoke only gasps, face flushed.

His reprieve from pain faded quickly, though. In a final spasm of agony, he doubled over, hands grasping his chest, crumpled to the floor, rolled to his side and then back, and just ceased moving. One last exhale evaporated into silence.

"Tanek? Tanek!" Grigory tried to revive his new friend from afar, but Tanek lay deadly still, his chest not moving. "Of course, the Polish capitalist dies of a heart attack before I had a chance to kill him. Fattened on greed, no doubt."

The living two animated the chamber with a shared sneer and eulogized the deceased with ideological quips from the past. The laughs soon subsided.

Wait. The game just changed.

Grigory raised his pistol for the win but missed the advantage by a split-second as the Czech socialist drew the same conclusion. Damn. "So, my fascist friend, we find ourselves in a new dilemma. As opposed to a few moments ago before our comrade died, now whoever shoots first lives, eh?"

Inhospitable Czech eyes acknowledged the challenge. This would be fun, no? A heart-pounding standoff followed. After so many hard years of life in small-city Russia, it was no longer called fear; it was fuel. The Rus slowly but steadily retreated until his heel pressed against the brick border. Pistol unwavering, he sidestepped toward the dead man's room. Like a reflection in a life-size mirror, Bara moved away from it until the two shooters stood as many paces from each other as possible; it wasn't far enough. Any firm grip and open eye could hit the target across these tiny rooms with these long barrels.

Clang, clang …

Both men startled at the sudden noise, triggering simultaneous gun blasts. Grigory watched his reflection jerk, spatter blood on the cinder, and lurch backwards as Grigory hit his own wall. A crimson hole ballooned in the same spot as his own throbbing pain. Blood spilled here; blood soaked the floor in the mirror image there. Both fell to their knees, both ...

8

House Meeting

"UGH. A HOUSE MEETING? That's messed up, Blue. We don't live here. We're not roomies." Red moped from the comfort of her bed and solitary thoughts to join their next brainstorming session, with no reason to expect a productive ending this time. The others already sat in the middle of the chamber. It's not like she could drown out the boys bickering anyway, but their ideas confused her because they all sounded promising. Her thoughts only reminded her of past mistakes, and nobody wanted those leftovers. Her previous escape plans never broke her out of school for a day nor out of the house for a night. She toted a pillow, but would not, however, bother with shoes.

She stopped halfway. "First, I need you two to turn away for a minute."

"Why?" Both men stared back, oblivious to her needs.

"Uh, because I need to use the bathroom, and I don't want you staring." Zero walls protected her privacy, but at least there was toilet paper.

"Of course, we will respect your modesty." Green's voice comforted her.

"Doesn't bother you that the entire world watches you pee?" Blue asked.

She hugged her pillow and looked up. Darkness still hovered just out of reach. They hadn't found any cameras yet—lamp, headboard, toilet seat, all clean—but who knew what lurked where they couldn't see? "I can't control that, so don't make me think about it. You, though ..." She pointed at them and twirled her index finger.

Blue and Green looked at each other, shrugged shoulders, and scooched around, leaning in and whispering among themselves. Let them have their jokes, as long as she didn't have to hear it and as long as they didn't peep. She had set a goal to only go once a day, and this was her time.

When done, she zipped up and gave the all clear. "Much better. The meeting may now resume. Thanks for at least not calling it a powwow this time, Blue."

"I'm still waiting for my first dance lesson. Can't schedule a powwow proper without a good dance off."

Still with the jokes, Blue? She shuffled to the limit of her world for the past week—maybe; tracking time with no clocks proved tricky—to the middle of the broader cavern where all three inmates met for the ritual stare up a soulless ladder that held the hope of life, though none saw the top. *What if it led nowhere?*

"Both boys brought their guns to a peaceful negotiation, of course." She tramped back to her dresser, pillow in tow, and returned better prepared for the armed parley, joining the others on the floor, cross-legged and hugging her pillow. A pungent scent arose from either it or her feet, or both, like old Cheetos. Moldy particles clung to her tongue.

"Take your finger off the trigger, please. It's not safe." Now Blue played a hall monitor in addition to a house mom. "Sorry, I'm just worried about you, about us all. Now, I have to ask again, has anyone figured a way out?"

Since nobody thought to hide a hand drill in their underwear before their abduction, no, nobody had a way out. An awkward silence hung for a few moments before he poked again. "I'm pretty sure I slapped every square centimeter of my walls and didn't feel a bump out of place. You?"

Two nods checked that item off the to-do list. *Progress, finally.* Maybe Blue would lighten up now.

"Any levers, pressure plates, air holes?"

Two shakes this time. "Any other thoughts?"

She stared at Green, hoping his imagination worked better than hers.

"If we can't escape, we should discuss a way to play the game." Green advocated for his main agenda, ranking who should live or die.

"We are; we're playing to win, though, not planning to lose." Blue stuck to his recent script, cooperation, even though that plot hadn't progressed much. "Speaking of losing, Willa, could you please keep your finger off your trigger? You're making me nervous."

She peeked down. Sure enough, her index finger poked through the trigger guard and caressed the mechanism that mattered. Aiming her firearm toward the ceiling, she left that finger on the trigger and raised the middle one in defiance. "There. Feel better now?"

A boyish grin replied.

"Is this a serious session, or are you two going to flirt the entire time?" Green, adding deadpan comedian to his stilted list of personality traits, used sarcasm to draw the conversation into his favorite topic—why he should win the game. He stood, a power move to raise his stature above hers. "I'm just saying, a species that flies across a galaxy can make an escape-proof prison. They are in charge here. We need to accept that."

Blue matched the testosterone level and rose in reply, ratcheting up the emotion. The serious discussion elevated to a passionate debate: two male wolves peeing sequentially on the same spot. "Fine, Rasheed. You have the floor. Why should you be the one to walk away ... alone?"

"Simple. My people contribute more to civilization. How about math? Morality? Manliness?"

Did he just glance and sneer at me? The slight compelled her to stand and argue too, leaving the pillow to rest on its own. "You're not the only one that matters, Green. We also matter to someone out there." She pointed up to the caliginous end of that ladder.

"It's not about me; it's about humanity's future." Green's voice strengthened. "All I'm saying is what value do your demographics bring to the world? That's what we must consider, how the world looks when two of our deaths cull the population. No?" He honed his impassioned homily.

Blue replied with equal fervor but higher volume. "Everyone's valuable." Arms swept a wide circle. Voice spilled out further, too. "Everyone in this freak cave deserves life."

It amazed her how easily people expressed their feelings. She felt emotions, sure, but conveying them to loved ones eluded her, except for yelling at her brother. That spewed easily. Maybe that's why she enjoyed writing. The process provided room to draft, revise, and hone her internals into a comprehensible message for the world to hear.

"It really upsets me when you two yell at each other. Stop arguing, just stop!" It was her dad and brother ruining her eighth-grade formal dance all over again.

She fled the tension and tripped. Hands whipped along the fall, slamming a firearm against rocky ground with a finger wrapped around the trigger.

Bang.

The deafening blast pounded her hearing and penetrated her head, viscous waves of muted noise bounced around, throbbing every second or two, soaking up all other sounds and converting them to dull pressure points against the skull. Wow, were those tight cave walls loud. Hands cupped and protected her eardrums, warm barrel against her head. When that pain passed, she rolled onto her side to witness Blue and Green in a standoff—guns pointed at each other with one hand while the other covered a single ear.

"What are you doing?" she screamed, compensating for the lingering ring.

"I don't know! Ask Green. I was checking on you and noticed him staring me down. Then he drew on me."

Green stiffened his stance, face still wincing in pain. "He pointed his gun at you. He was taking advantage of you being unarmed."

"Okay, let's all calm down. Thank you for the backup, Green, but if you kill Blue, what's that mean for you and me? We are both defenseless at that point."

The silence of the next several seconds validated the point. She stayed down, avoiding any sudden moves. Blue swayed, jittery. Green stood steady, steely eyed.

Ting.

Two pairs of male eyes shifted just enough to keep each other in sight, but also to search for the source of the tiny sound. She, in turn, scanned her surroundings, reached, and retrieved a brand-new bullet from the ground.

Gun held high and release pressed, a short, stiff jerk slid out the mag that glided into her other waiting hand. She slipped in the single, shiny round, slapped the mag back in place, and released the slide—finger prominently off the trigger.

"Back to stalemate, roomies."

A mountain of manmade instability leaned against Blue's wall, daring him to climb. His rickety desk on its side formed the base. Higher up, the long end of his bedframe aimed toward the darkness, buoyed by a twice-folded mattress, crumpled blanket and sheets, pencil drawer, and upside-down desk chair. The lamp rested on the desk's elevated side.

He both admired and feared his creation, and now he needed to conquer it. His idea, his risk. Explore the overhead shadows. Find an escape.

"You got this, Blue. Believe in yourself."

Easier said than done. Wiping sweat from his temple, he glanced at Red. She stood safely on her side of the bars, arms crossed and biting her lower lip. Green kneeled on one knee. One arm rested on his leg and propped his chin as he coached Blue through the dangerous maneuver.

A deep inhale while arms raised above his head and slow exhale while they lowered calmed his mind, as did a silent prayer. He hopped, planted palms on the desk, and pushed his body up. The mound wobbled.

"Careful," Red admonished.

"It'll hold." Green's prediction was not comforting.

After grabbing the lamp, he clenched the bedrails and checked their firmness against the wall. It didn't wiggle too much, so he climbed the bed's crossrails. Feet halfway up that makeshift ladder bumped his head against the darkness. The unseen, the unknown, hovered above. For the life of him, he couldn't figure out where the light originated. Fear warned him to retreat. Pride pushed him onward. He gingerly probed with the lamp. Nothing but air, so he climbed another rung. The entire contraption rattled.

A roomie gasped, probably not Green since he was too callous to care.

He froze until firm again. A faint buzz broke through the silence that followed.

"Great progress, Blue. Keep going." That was Green.

"Shush! Do you hear that?"

Several moments of quiet passed before Green replied. "No, what is it?"

"I don't know. Surging electricity, maybe? Beehive, maybe?"

"If it's bees, don't poke them with your lamp. Trust me." Good advice from Red. "I'll tell you that story later. In fact, if it's electricity, don't poke that either."

He hadn't come this far to quit and needed a better sense of what lurked above, a human touch. Taking a moment to survey his surroundings from his bird's-eye view, he decided against climbing down only to risk the trip up again. So, he leaned his head against the cold, stone wall for balance while he removed his dress shirt, the clothes he wore to his interview-slash-abduction. His white undershirt was no longer smooth nor clean.

"There's the beast we need," Green mocked from his comfortable position. "Flex 'em if you got 'em, Blue."

Wrapping a hand protected it from both of his scary guesses. This next reach into the inky air bumped nothing solid, but swept his bare arm through a warm spot, like a monster's hot breath.

"Whoa!"

He jerked. His mountain jiggled. The bundled mattress slipped backward, whisking the bottom of the bedframe along for the ride like a house on a mudslide. Eyes clenched shut, he screeched a duet with the metal scraping stone down the wall until the bedframe slammed flat on the desk. Tottering legs lost balance. He whacked the concrete, launching into a roll, ending with a scraped face to the floor.

Red shouted an ominous warning. "Don't move."

He opened his eyes mere centimeters from buzzing bars. Too close.

"You okay?" she asked.

"No," he moaned, "but on the bright side, I didn't get electrocuted again."

Blue's mind floated in that half-jittery state between fear and excitement. His homegrown ramp up the wall mocked him again, reminding him of his failed attempts so far to find the ceiling of their cell. Repeat the same steps and hope for a different outcome. "You know the definition of insanity, right?"

"Insanity. Noun. Using Blue's ideas to escape an alien game show. Now climb. It'll hold." Admittedly, Green's design improvement held promise. Blue would have to cut him some slack at their next house meeting.

Same sideways desk, same bunched mattress, but this time piled next to the buzzing border with Green's room and the wooden pencil drawer wedged between two bars. Green held his side, forming a lever that—theoretically—prevented the bottom of the leaning bedframe from sliding. Time to test.

What Blue lacked in confidence, he compensated for by forcing a bold face. He coiled his rolled-up sheet around his shoulder like a rope and gingerly lifted one leg onto the first rung of the bedframe ladder. It jittered. He raised the other foot level with the first. One by one, rail by rail, breath by breath, he climbed.

When feet reached as far as he dared, he slid the sheet rope off his shoulder. One end tied around the plastic bowl, for weight, from his daily meal that he never saw delivered. The other was knotted to keep the sheet from unraveling. Uncoiling and dangling the first loop, he gently swung the bowl in a circle, gaining momentum until he released it upward a meter.

Green scoffed. "Is that the best you got?"

Blue huffed. "No, dude. That was a test. I'm starting slow until I figure out how stable my ladder is."

"Good idea." Red golf-clapped her approval.

"Just throw. It'll hold."

"Says the guy with his feet on solid ground." She supported Blue from her safe distance.

"That's what I'm saying. Thank you." He nodded his appreciation. "Now, I will throw it harder. Everyone quiet so we can hear what it hits." He swirled the bowl faster and launched it higher. It ascended and returned in silence except for the bedframe shuddering.

"Anything?" Red asked from meters away.

"Nothing. Trying again." A speedier swing and more forceful fling extended the sheet as far as it would stretch, yet still clunked nothing but air. No hot-breathed monster took the bait. The mound shook. Still grasping the sheet, he gripped the bedrail with both hands while the bowl sunk past and plinked the desk.

"Careful." Red couldn't help from her room, nor could she administer first aid if he tumbled and hurt himself.

He stood all alone atop his mountain, like he did at age six, trembling at the top of a ladder. Below, his brothers cackled and teased, sometimes shaking the base to force him to move higher.

He took a moment to recoup and return to the present. "Did I ever tell you my frisbee story?"

"I like stories," Red replied.

"First time I learned to throw one, it landed on the roof of our house. My brothers made me climb a rickety ladder, another first in my life, to retrieve it. Man, that thing bowed and wobbled, slid along the rain gutters. From the top, it looked so much higher than peeking out a second-story window." He leaned forward, closer to the wall, a little buzz forming in his head. "The higher I climbed, the smaller my brothers looked, like I could drop on top of their heads and nail them into the ground, you know, like in an anime."

"Funny visual." Red seemed to enjoy the tale.

He chuckled. "Yeah, but not at the time. I froze at the top of that ladder for an hour before swinging my leg around enough to step onto the roof. Then getting back onto the ladder, oh boy! Cruel punishment for a small kid who never tossed a disc before."

"Hey, Blue." Red's voice floated gently.

"Yeah?"

"Did you get the frisbee down?"

He swiveled his head to peer across the cavern. She stood close to the prison bars, arms crossed, nibbling on a thumbnail.

"Yeah, I did."

"And you'll find out what's buzzing up there, too, and you'll get down safely. Then we'll figure a way out of here, yeah?"

His dizziness disappeared.

Green held the pencil drawer steady. "That's right, Blue. I got you. Bed's not going anywhere. Hear anything?"

"Nothing." Frustrating.

"Try tossing the rope to the side toward the bars. See if it reaches over the top. Maybe they don't go that high."

"Good idea, Green." Red's voice signaled the thumbs-up approval.

He spun and slung. Cushioned plastic clinked metal. For one final, valiant attempt, he whipped the bowl, letting go of the sheet to fly as high as puny muscles could propel it. The momentum shook his precarious pile. Dress shoes slipped off their footholds. He grabbed for the sides but slid down, his head thunking against steel and thudding the concrete—again.

"Oh my God, are you alright?" Red yelped.

The wrapped bowl bonked the floor beside his head and the sheet rope drifted down. He groaned for both his back and his pride while slapping the floor. Another failure to add to the growing list.

Green held up the pencil drawer. "For the record, the pencil drawer held, as predicted."

"I told you; I'm done." Blue rubbed his sore lower back. He stared at Green, resolute that he had climbed his last shaky mountain. Let Green take the next risk.

Red fidgeted in her room, one arm holding her opposite elbow. "Don't look at me. I didn't make the rock-paper-scissors rules."

"Don't all natives grow up climbing trees looking for coconuts or something?" Green asked, concerned eyes returning to the challenge bars facing him. "This should be second nature for you."

"Uh, pretty sure you're thinking of Polynesians." She corrected Green's geography with the same sarcastic tone and eye roll she used to eventually teach Blue that Lisbon was, in fact, *not* a suburb of Barcelona. Beauty, brains, and a bit of a bite when proved right.

Green sighed and peered upward. Sheets bound a pillow to each of his raised forearms, like rectangular foam fingers cheering himself to victory. The pillows covered his hands, too.

"You got this, Rasheed. Ra-sheed. Ra-sheed." Blue chanted, psyching up his roomie.

Red joined the cheer, arms pumping the air. "Ra-sheed. Ra-sheed."

Green huffed and puffed, soaking in deeper and deeper breaths. He stepped back, stuttered his feet, and roared as he slammed both pillows against the electrified bars and held them tight.

Nothing buzzed.

Three harrowing seconds later, he jumped back and laughed. "Ha! It worked."

Blue clapped and celebrated his great idea. "Told you. I told you it'd be fine. Pillows are an insulator. Now scale that wall and rescue us."

A beaming Green repeated his pre-climb psych-out routine, jogged and jumped this time, and pressed his protected forearms and hands onto the bars. Shoes planted against them as well. Still no sizzle, so he shimmied. Huff and puff, left and right, hands and feet shuffled higher until his head pierced the dark. Soon, the skyless night hid him from waist up.

"Uh, uh oh. No, no." Green stammered.

"What? What's wrong? We can't see you." He shuffled, ducked, leaned all around for a better view.

"It's slipping off."

A pillow fell from the sky like a fluffy meteor followed by a crack of lightning.

Zap.

Green screamed as he plummeted, shoes and one still-attached pillow slowing his descent like wet brakes. Feet pounded the floor and he rolled backward, moaning. After a moment, he recovered his footing, rubbed the back of his head, and kicked the helpless pillow. "Ya kalb! You dog."

"Are you hurt?" Red's eyes peeked from behind protective hands.

"Of course I'm hurt, ya sharmouta. I nearly died."

He did not need a degree in Arabic to sense how pissed Green was, so he bit his tongue and let Green wander his room, vent, swear, and walk off the shock.

They could try again tomorrow.

9

Just Playing by the Rules

Gang Fan—nighttime construction worker turned round-the-clock internet celebrity—peered over his cold shoulder and glowered at his Japanese cellmate. Gang sat in front of a computer screen, stuck in a conversation with his aging father who couldn't stop recounting his dad's stories from the long-ago war. He got it; life was cruel. As Grandfather told it, those island devils brought evil across the water to Chinese shores, and by the time they left, untold tens-of-thousands of innocents lay dead or mutilated.

As the elder son, Gang had accomplished little in life except repeatedly driving father to sorrow. No wife, no child, and a failed concrete pouring business, but now he eyed his once-in-a-lifetime opportunity to honor the family name and exact revenge. Patriots would surely take care of his family out of gratitude.

"Goodbye, Baba. Tell little brother to keep an eye on this room's statistics, then you rest in peace."

He rose and tucked gun under belt before stretching a stiff neck. A breezeless chill skimmed his skin. He strode to the center where two other male strangers whispered while glancing up a ladder leading to the night, all three abductees separated by prison bars that stretched from an outer cave wall to a ring of bars surrounding the ladder. The conversation fled as he arrived, leaving him to his silent assessment. No other decision in his life presented so loudly, so clearly. He was a CEO again, making tough decisions that affected other people's lives for his benefit.

One stranger mattered to Gang's scheme, but the other, the nervous black devil, spoke first with a broken but direct dialect, baritone voice punching out staccato notes. "Hello. Do you speak English?"

Gang nodded and still stared at the third man, a clean-cut, working class elder with thin-rimmed glasses and eyes slanted the wrong way.

"Good. I am Tula, from Zimbabwe. This is Benjiro, from Tokyo. His English is not so good."

The dongyang guizi, that east ocean devil, bowed his head.

Gang soaked in a deep breath. A numbing peace relaxed his muscles.

Tula continued. "Do you know where we are, why we are here? Can you believe what the computer tells us?"

Gang sighed, clicked his tongue, and rolled his neck. Time to act. "Yes, I believe. The strong have no reason to lie." With that, he drew his pistol, aimed at Benjiro's chest just two meters away, and killed him.

Gang's head thundered from the blast as Tula recoiled.

After the piercing reverberations cleared, the shooter dropped his gun, slide locked back longing for another round, and looked at his one living cellmate. The deed done; the soul still numb.

In the silence of two stares, a clanging arose from around the ladder. He observed not one but three separate rings of bars surrounded the escape route. Each ring did not form a full circle, though, only two-thirds of one, leaving a one-third gap—an open gate—aligned with the vee formed by two walls of bars that met at the ladder. The net result was two layers of fencing between each prisoner's cell and the way out, not three. As the clanging continued, though, one of those rings rotated, moving its gap to align with Tula's room, leaving just one layer of fencing blocking his way to freedom.

"You see that, Tula? Kill me, and the final fence will spin, granting you access to go."

The bright white of Tula's eyes nearly popped out of his pitch-black face. "You know your people die, too?"

He smirked. "Did you talk with your family? Our conquerors do not care about race, but we do. I am a Han Chinese who just wiped out thousands of Tokyo Japanese. Plus,"—he shrugged shoulders and spread his arms, palms facing out, accepting silent cheers from an unseen audience—"I live in Ho Chi Minh City, so today I win twice."

The avenging angel smiled contently. The final trigger clicked, muzzle flashed, powder cracked, and a round pounded his chest. He expected the thud of the floor, but blackness fell first.

Tula stared down his gun's barrel for an eternity, both hands clenched the grip. No bodies stirred. No breath lingered. Stillness reigned. Eventually, that next partial ring clanged and spun until the final one-third gap opened toward his room, removing all metal between him and the ladder. He holstered his weapon and shuffled forward, gingerly testing the rails for shocks before grasping one. His climb sped up as he rose higher from the ground until he hit the darkness. What felt like a final kilometer took what seemed a lifetime. Each hand patted the emptiness above before finding and grasping the next rung until he finally clunked a circular hatch, which he turned and pushed. Daylight flooded his eyes with radiant freedom.

The hatch swung open and thudded to the ground. His head emerged in a small field on the edge of a residential area, welcoming sunshine high in the sky. Shiny apartment buildings housing beautiful families and home cooking dotted his view just blocks away while scattered high rises filled the background. A soccer ball whizzed past, playful. He turned to find tan-skinned, black-haired children staring at him. Southeast Asia. Climbing the last steps and kissing the grass dancing in the breeze, the Zimbabwean replied with an ear-to-ear grin to the horns and machinery hums all accepting him back into civilization.

He waved to the children. "Hello. Do you speak English?"

From pitch black moonless night to blinding day, a single light flooded Tula's eyes once someone removed the hood from his head. Rough ropes trapped his wriggling hands behind the chair back. Dank mildew irritated his nose. Though it had cost him a chunk of his soul, he thought he had miraculously survived the harrowing one-bullet dilemma room and was free. Now what?

"Hello? Who is there?" Tula discerned no shapes.

A throat cleared. Papers shuffled. The scene slowly filled in from the edges—a tiny room furnished with just that light, a table, one occupied seat behind, and his chair exposed in the middle. Only the seams around thick shades outlined two windows. A cigarette lit. The lighter's glow fell softly on a Vietnamese face behind the table, who blew smoke past the indoor sun, tangy tobacco scent blending with the background musk.

"Tula, right? From Zimbabwe."

"Yes. Who are you?" He scraped his feet across concrete.

His interrogator balanced a cigarette on the edge of an ashtray, raised a huge hunting knife, examined it, started twirling it, carving figure eights in the air around his wrists. "You are a long way from home, about nine-thousand kilometers. Do you miss it?"

"I have done nothing wrong. Release me."

"Nothing wrong?" The inquisitor leaped to his feet, chair grinding backwards, and sunk the blade into the desktop with a thunk. "You killed hundreds of thousands of people in an instant. A third are from this city. Everyone watched the game statistics jump when you pulled your trigger, watched the map of their country light up blue as alien oppressors exchanged the money they gambled, and now every family is waiting for a loved one to disappear. Everyone knows your face, Tula. It is difficult for an African to blend into Ho Chi Minh

City. What do you think the grieving families will do when they find you? Let you just sail away?"

Nervous sweat dripped onto lips. "That was not my fault; I had no choice."

The Vietnamese snatched the knife and stomped to the Zimbabwean, planting hands on chair arms. Stern eyes stared into scared ones, intimidating. A cold blade tapped against bare arms. He slinked around the seat, out of sight; steel slid along skin. The captor tugged on the binding ropes and loosed the knot, freeing Tula's hands.

The liberator now gripped Tula's arms, jerked him to his feet, and dragged him to a covered window, cracking the shade.

Outside, a vexed crowd scurried about a shopping district. A woman wailed across the street, head leaning against a wall. A gang of men thrashed around in a full-on melee, blocking traffic. A baseball bat shattered a storefront window.

"There's a rumor that someone spotted a black man in this neighborhood. Imagine what happens if I open that door and yell, 'found him.' Door's unlocked. Walk away if you want, but right now, Tula, I'm your only friend."

"What do you want with me? Who are you?"

"You'll never need my name, but you need my help, and I want information. I can get you home, alive. Can anyone else offer that? Your company, perhaps? Or maybe this guy outside burning a Zimbabwean flag? Oh, he looks mad, doesn't he? If you ever hope to see family again, to feel Zimbabwe's soil between your toes, I need to know everything you know about your OBD, the one-bullet dilemma room. Everything, starting with where it is."

Knife still dangling, the negotiator sauntered to his cigarette and drew another breath through his filter while Tula rubbed his raw wrists.

"So, Tula. Should I find safe passage on a boat, or open that door and walk away?"

Climb out of one hellhole, wind up in another.

"There, in the middle of the field. The hatch is closed now."

Pham Xuan An, Ho Chi Minh City resistance leader and tough-as-necessary interrogator, peered through a crack in the van's curtains as Tula pointed to an inconspicuous hole in the ground highlighted by a late-afternoon sun. The rest of the Vietnamese resistance movement's first squad peeked through other windows hunting for collaborators, anyone too interested in the plain patterns of this urban setting to live or work there. The live feed from the room darkened soon after Gang Fan hit the floor, but Pham knew that did not mean the enemy wouldn't monitor its prized asset. He needed intel on these hellholes, and Tula represented his best opportunity. This op was worth the risk.

In Vietnamese, he directed his three squads. "Two, this is One; park on the other side of the field. Three, patrol a two-block radius. If we are spotted, do not engage. Split up and rendezvous at zone one. I do not have to remind you the ten of us are the only resistance left. No matter what, we must survive."

In English, he threatened the African informant with his stare and reminded him of the pecking order. "I told my people that *we* must survive, Tula, not necessarily you. Don't do anything stupid."

He then cracked open the side door and assessed the surrounding block, eyeing no threats. Three teenagers leaned against a nearby railing, eyes pinned to phones. He whistled and waved a few bills, drawing one close enough to talk over the noise of passing traffic.

"Yeah, that's the room. We climbed down, but there's nothing left inside. They must have cleared out the beds and dressers that first night after the black man left, but we never saw anyone come or go. The two bodies are still there, though. They stink, bad."

Ah, humans poking around the OBD never triggered a response. Good. He paid for the information, grabbed gear, and gestured for one comrade to follow. "Get in. Recon. Get out."

Looking like the next round of disappointed grave robbers, the two donned facemasks for the stench and climbed a few meters down the ladder. No light except their flashlights and a single shaft of sunbeam fell on anything inside. Fine dust flakes lingered in the air. Dangling from the side rail, he let fly two mango-size mapping drones while he scanned the roof and walls.

"There." Cameras stuck out from the rock wall in Tula's room right where expected based on angles used during the deadly game show.

Once on the ground and in the only accessible room, the other soldier unlashed a collapsible titanium ladder from his pack. After extending it from its one-meter packed length to its full three meters, he leaned it against the wall. The soldier planted his foot at the base to grip it steady on the smooth floor while Pham climbed high. The extra height placed face and flashlight level with the camera, embedded as if the rock formed around it.

A meter above the camera, a meter-wide band of metal encircled the entire room. Its dull finish blended well with the wall. In the silence, a faint second hum joined the buzzing drones. He raised a hand closer. It sank into a patch of warmer air in front of that band.

Balancing precariously and returning to task, he eyed and poked every centimeter around the camera until he found a removable faceplate. A gingerly procured multi-tool pried it off, uncoiling power and fiberoptic cables from behind. He pinned electronic trackers through their shielding, rewound the wires, and replaced the plate.

Feet back on solid ground, foulness of rotting flesh penetrating their masks, the two reconned the barren room, as empty as ruins of extinct civilizations deep in the jungle. They retrieved the mapping drones and re-climbed to the exit. As their vans drove away, Pham called his contact inside the utility company, and in code tasked him with searching for the signal from the trackers he stuck into the camera cables.

"Yeah, there's a problem with my internet," and he rattled off a nearby address to narrow the search grid. "Yes, a full modem test, please. Call me back when you figure it out."

After hanging up, he tapped the driver's shoulder. "To the port." He leaned back and spoke to the African. "Thank you, Tula. As promised, we'll load you on a cargo ship and contact your friend with the itinerary. Once we drop you off in Somalia, though, you are on your own. I wish you luck getting home. Oh, one more thought. Just like we helped you, a stranger who killed thousands of us, you should consider how to help the world get out of this mess. You're a celebrity now. Use that."

10

Red's Cold. Green's Vision

*U*GH, *I HATE COLDS.* Not only did Red's body ache all over, but her caretakers also sent no tissues to accompany the lack of napkins with every daily meal. Before she knew it, one edge of her bedsheet filled with mucus. Disgusting. Misery longed for company, but when she rose to force Blue to commiserate with her at their shared border, she met solid rock all around, walling off both Blue's and Green's room. Her cosmos had shrunk by two-thirds.

"What the hell?"

With both a stained sheet and torn blanket wrapped around her body and head, she trekked toward the cliff, afraid to reach out in case it still shocked the innocent like the bars that used to stand guard there. A stare upward to drain sinuses and an epiphany to solve the problem returned her to her metal-backed, rolling office chair, which she unceremoniously flung into the stone wall. No sparks flew, but shockingly, as the chair bounced off and rolled away, the rock faded into familiar bars. On the other side, with eyes closed and fingers inter-twined as if praying fervently, Blue swatted empty air as if chasing a giant fly. After some swings, he opened his eyes and looked surprised to see Red instead of a bug. Goof.

"Oh, hey, Willa. Looks like I'm back. Shoot, I didn't get to finish the sim."

"Sim?"

"Yeah, a hyper-realistic historical simulation with sights, sounds, pain, swords, smell of burning flesh ..." The excitement in his voice made a creepy match with the description.

She stood aloof, swaddled head tilted back, peering at an unseen ceiling.

He continued. "... but apparently we have more exciting wonders to ponder."

"Huh? Yeah, I'm listening. Sim, pain, etcetera. All very exciting, Blue. I'm just dealing with this friggin' head cold. So annoying."

"Did you eat? I can never remember, does eating help a cold? What's on your menu today?"

Shuffling to her desk, she rubbed above her eyebrows, the worst of the pressure, sniffled, and risked un-tilting her dripping head to check her tray. "Meatloaf. I can't smell it, but I'm sure it's disgusting. You?"

"Mmm. Jackpot. Beef stew, chunks of potato, thick carrots. Smells divine."

"Oh, you dirty dog. Beef stew is my fav. Why would they give *you* my favorite dish?"

"Seriously?" Blue swiveled his head, eyeing his dinner and then her.

Oh, no. Did she have a pitiful look that screamed for charity? Probably, but it was beef stew.

"Ah- ... ahh- ..." The jokester feigned a toxic sneeze aimed right at her taste buds' desire, but ended the ruse before the punchline. Not funny. "I know exactly why they gave me your favorite dish, and I for one am not playing their sick game any longer, no pun intended. Give me a minute to think."

He studied his meager possessions, fluffing pillows, pulling out empty drawers, scrutinizing them, then replacing each with a sigh, like an eighth-grade girl picking out her clothes for the party the high schoolers invited her to. He settled on the blanket.

"Fortunately, the bowl is plastic, ergo—like my big word, Miss Master's Degree?" The blanket rolled into a long, crumpled log.

"Pfft. Don't hurt yourself, Mr. Mere Bachelor's."

"Ergo, the plastic bowl will slip under the zapping wall of zapping zaps with no issues." The crumpled log folded in half, forming a tight vee.

"I have no idea what you're saying."

"Watch and be amazed." He set the food on the floor near the electrified prison bars. With the point of the vee pressed against the bowl, hands safely back half a meter holding the open ends, he nudged that steaming, satisfying stew to her side, phantom smell triggering deep in her memory.

"Are you being serious right now?"

"It's your *fav*, right? I'll trade you for the meatloaf, after you eat." Problem solved, cocky Blue retreated toward his bed, perfectly dressed for the party.

"Well ... want to sit together and chat while we eat?"

The bargain struck, she copied Blue's blanket solution and slid her slab of yuck his way, then leaned back on the rock wall near the metal one between them while devouring the best stew in memory that she couldn't fully taste, warming cocoon of bedding again wrapped around body and head.

"Let me ask you something." Blue finished chewing. "Day one, when we first learned about our little dilemma, you froze for a minute, had a faraway gaze going. What were you thinking about?"

She slowed her munching while her mind tasted that bitter memory again. Eyes stared at nothing.

"Death, sort of. Oblivion, I suppose. Mostly, though, I thought I'm going to die here alone, and there's nobody who will miss me."

"Come on. Nobody? No family, no boyfriend?"

"Nope. Dad passed away. I have a brother, somewhere, maybe. I suppose if he ever sobers up, he may miss me."

Chews filled the silence until she cleared her throat. "Am I so sick I'm hallucinating, or is there a rock wall all around Green's room now? You had one, too."

"You're not crazy; it's there. Best guess is this prevents us from killing him while he's vulnerable in his holo-sim."

"How do they make solid rock just appear?"

"Pfft. I can't even make beef stew. No way I know that answer."

"What's he experiencing right now?"

"No clue, but I'm sure he's enjoying it."

Green woke abruptly from a deep sleep, jarred by clanging metal and screaming people. This was not the chamber.

Black ash and white smoke floated across his view of a daytime sky. A burning ember landed on his arm. His scream rose, joined the others from the crowd, and drowned in the riptides of anguish all about. He rolled to his side and swept the hot spot over and over until the chunk of glowing wood fell away, leaving behind a broiled piece of flesh. The scent of melted skin permeating the air reeked more than just his minor burn.

Men, women, and children that looked like him rushed in every direction but one, chaos unleashed. The fields strewn with bodies left in the wake of the swirling violence, some moaning and crawling minus one of their limbs, others lying still like peaceful babies sleeping. Many smoldered like the village houses dotting the distance.

He didn't remember how he wound up here, but then again, he hadn't remembered getting to the chamber that first night.

One mother twenty meters away carrying a bawling toddler careened toward him, then launched the child with outstretched arms while she fell with a thud, a thick arrow sticking straight in the air from her lifeless body.

The child writhed in pain.

In the billows of smoke behind them emerged a platoon of kafir soldiers, unscathed chain mail glinting in the mourning sun; pointed helmets circled their brows, with nose guards protruding from iron rims. The unbroken square formation slinked forward, swinging swords splashing unarmored blood and skin to the angry wind.

Step by step they killed and maimed their way toward helpless Green. The history of his people, taught to him but unheard by him as a child, now surrounded him in living color, dying sounds, and suffocating scents.

Tall shields that nearly covered the attacker's entire bodies easily ridiculed every attempt to slow their approach. They came for him; they salivated for him to suffer. Every sword that didn't cut down his kin pointed at him.

The thump in his chest and quickened breaths tingled his skin and clouded his mind. He was far from his lamb dinners and wine tastings with clients, and he didn't know what to do.

A conqueror's flag with a white backdrop applauded in the wind from the center of the square. *Clap ... clap ... clap.* Next to it, a familiar face barked evil orders like a dog, commanding each advance, ordering each death, warning of each threat, laughing at each dismemberment.

It was Blue. *I knew I couldn't trust him.*

A squad of brave defenders clothed in colorful tunics charged to Green and kneeled to form a protective line, vengeful arrows already nocked. Each drew their bow, aimed at the masochists, and let fly their righteous fury.

Mocking laughter echoed as arrow after arrow thudded off those tall shields emblazoned with a single symbol, crimson like the blood that watered the battlefield.

A return volley from invisible cowards inside their impenetrable iron defenses blanketed the sky, implanting in grass and bone alike. One hit Green's tunic below his armpit, missing his heart by a handbreadth, pinning him to the ground. He tugged, tearing the cloth, but the shaft barely shook.

All but one of his people fell.

The lone survivor bolted to Green and freed him from his wooden captor. "Your business was impressive, my friend. Too bad the foreigners always cheat, but you can still make a name for yourself. Remember your people. Remember your brothers. Remember this day. If you exact revenge in fifty years, you acted too soon. Now flee and live."

He then wielded his small shield, drew his short sword, and stormed the encroaching danger with a ferocious battle cry.

Confused by what his struggling business had to do with all this, Green still heeded his savior's last advice and raced for his life. That option made sense. His burned arm stung as he pushed himself up. Heavy legs stumbled across the field as he dodged listless bodies. An arrow sunk into the ground in front of his path. He had to run faster in order to live.

As the sounds of steel and stench of ancient war faded behind, a steel and glass high rise formed in front of his eyes. Pixels of muted colors emerged from thin air and coalesced into a shining structure, building it many stories high. The safety of the front glass doors welcomed him in but locked behind. The second set, also transparent, barred his entry into the lobby. They trapped him just outside of modernity.

Behind the central reception desk, dual white staircases unfolded like angel wings, one from each of the honorable scribes. Two trains of women flowed from the second floor. Dozens descended from the left flights, some layered with hijabs, some in niqabs, others in burqas. From the right decline stepped a matching feminine column, some in animal skin skirts, some in tasseled cloth leggings, others topless save for a few feathers of long war bonnets draped over light-brown shoulders. The processions crossed in front of the clear doors blocking his path until the rows covered the entire entrance beyond the glass, just out of reach but within clear sight. His sisters and nieces stood in front, each with a paired savage stationed behind, some with faces decorated in streaks of black ash, some in red dots and white stripes, others with unpainted skin. Now that they stood closer, he recognized the back row all as copies of Red—intense, dark eyes with immoral intent staring him down.

Each clone unsheathed a flint knife and clamped the foreheads of those in front while slowly slashing the cloth necks of hijabs and burqas. Psychotic Red enjoyed that too much.

He shuddered the door handles, but they would not submit.

No skin sliced open, no blood flowed, but it may as well have since the clean cuts dropped all protective clothing to the floor, revealing shameful breasts, immodest hips, and corrupted thighs of an entire generation. As if the insult was not sharp enough, Red dug the stone blade deeper into his psyche. Up and down the whole parade, she kissed the necks and caressed the waists of her partners, eliciting acceptance and desire from left to right.

He closed his eyes and wept.

"Stop corrupting my people, please!"

He pounded on the glass barricade over and over until it shattered; his anger made a difference. From the bottom floor up, man-sized shards formed and separated from the entire building, falling and crashing to the ground, disappearing into fine glints of dust. After the building vanished, the bright skies and green grass vaporized, wasting away from the heavens down to the earth, darkening as they fled into familiar, dismal chamber walls.

He was back, kneeling by his bed, arms overhead to protect him from the imploding scene, screaming and weeping in anguish. His fellow prisoners looked on with disdain from the other side of iron sticks. Annoying Blue dared to speak.

"Welcome back, buddy. How was your day trip?"

11
Crappy Assignment

RAFIQ SLOGGED THROUGH A sewer tunnel flowing waist high with liquid denser than a gentle river, headlamp lighting the way. Clumps of solid stuff bumped against his thighs, protective waders still thin enough to convey those reminders that he did not tread in fresh waters. A crappy assignment, for sure. Each step against the resistive fluid worked chunky legs harder than his last visit to a gym a few resolutions ago—like walking through sludge. Nobody's fault but his own.

Maybe this new pastime as a resistance fighter was the motivation he needed to get back in shape. First mission: locate the local one-bullet dilemma room so the good guys could shut it down, and don't get caught. His daughter would never understand, and his wife would never forgive.

A terrible reek hung as thick and oppressive as the pressing water. Wireless earbuds drowned out the slosh while recent hours of footage from that local OBD projected inside his glasses, a pleasant distraction.

"In another life, it'd be wonderful for Red and Blue to get together. They'd make a cute couple." Rafiq spoke to himself to ease his tension, pass the time, and guarantee someone laughed at his jokes.

A distant clunk echoed down the tube.

"Oh. Clever, Blue, pushing beef stew under the bars with a blanket. Now, help me figure a way to get you all out of that disgusting room." A feeder pipe poured more goop from the left.

The show fan paused his video player, climbed a short ladder, switched off his light, and cracked open the sealed roof hatch. After scanning for nearby activity, he poked his head through and surveyed the utilidor, the utility corridor that housed his one-man cylindrical highway plus miles of racks filled with pipes carrying cleaner water, fiberoptic cables, and power lines. Nobody else roamed that section, but distant flashlights flickered. He relaxed and took the quiet moment to calm his breath. In no time, the lights faded. Probably power guys ending their shift. Back to alone.

He finished the climb out, flipped his headlamp to the low-power red light, stepped to a maintenance panel, and pulled test gear from under waterproof waders. After jacking in, he smiled at the stronger readings, which meant he didn't have to backtrack the few hundred meters and try a different direction.

"Praise."

His phone buzzed. "Hi, Leeew-yaaa-I-mean random stranger whose name I am not using on an open channel ... Yes, I'm closer, north of our previous reading ... I don't know how much farther. Your Vietnamese friend just gave us frequencies, not signal strengths. Best we can do is move toward stronger ones ... Yes, I'll report back soon."

The Vietnamese resistance—a concerned neighbor half-way around the globe—fed intel to the not-random stranger on the phone who in turn recruited Rafiq to search the sprawling sewers under the busy Charlotte, North Carolina streets. Armed with the power signature from the Ho Chi Minh City OBD room—definitely phase-shifted for nefarious purposes—Rafiq's local resistance aimed to rescue the unwitting from their murderous destiny and stab the heart of the enemy's greatest advantage.

The humble utility worker understood absolutely nothing about guerilla warfare or counter-occupation movements, probably couldn't spell the words, but faith colored his perception of genocide, especially of his own people. Inaction equaled compliance. However, he understood hitting the enemy where it hurt, and he knew the stinky sewers. He had no clue how to grip a gun either, let alone shoot one. If resistance duties came down to that, he'd drop the weapon, crack a joke, and accept fate. Nothing happens that was not meant to be.

After the call, he switched gear to the fiber optic panel to test a side theory. Power went to the room, but data had to flow, too, at least for the video. He wiped a speck from the monitor, but it didn't move. "Huh." He upped his game by licking his thumb and taking another swipe. Still not clear, so he lifted and angled it to catch a better glint from his headlamp. It wasn't dirt; it was a tiny signal on the edge of the grid lines. A knob click widened the range, revealing a second signature, high frequency and ultra-wideband. A fun little discovery.

"Ah, interesting. Let's record these readings and examine you later." He hid his spare gear behind the conduit and closed the panel. He'd retrieve it in a few days on his next sweep.

After packing up, he stood at the hatch back into the sewer, longing headlamp beam tracing the clean utilidor floor in his next direction. That route was faster, sure, smelled better, too, but more prone to cross paths with utility workers who'd like to know why strangers were messing around their lines. Avoid those people, avoid those questions, which meant no avoiding the climb down.

He hit play on his show as he humped through the next stretch of slush.

"Oo, a historical holo-sim for Green? Wonder why the aliens do that?"

Perhaps it's pure entertainment. Or could have been experiments, their version of rats in a maze. *Oo, maybe it was a product demonstration. Show our leaders what tech they get in return for sanctioning these hellholes.*

He bounced ideas around as chunks bounced off his thighs. One more hour, and he should be done.

12

Time For a New Plan

"**S**ERIOUSLY, RASHEED. IT'S BEEN two days since your hologram vision. What did you see?"

Blue sat cross-legged on the hard floor close to the buzzing metal hedge, trying to converse with Green. Only silence replied, which frazzled Blue's nerves.

"It's interesting the meal you keep neglecting to eat stays there and isn't replaced when ours are, don't you think? Smells like rotisserie chicken. I'll bet it's delicious." Blue kept his voice low to not disturb sleeping beauty, but still raspy enough to reach across the third room. She lay in her bed along with her desk tilted on its side and facing outward.

The food inquiry fell on deaf ears. Green just sat in his bed, back to the stone perimeter, gun-toting arm propped on a bent knee, daring anyone to approach. He kept cocking and closing the hammer, up and down. *Click*, cocked. *Click*, closed. And he kept examining his arm, stroking the smooth hair and skin that appeared completely normal to Blue.

The inquisitor kept at it. "Did you know that when you enter your hologram these prison bars turn into solid stone around your room?"

No reply to that revelation, though eventually Green shared his vision.

"I saw … they showed me why I should hate you both. Guess they don't trust me to figure it out myself. Great clashes between civilizations in the past, and a great clash of ideas today. Immorality then and now." *Click*. "Bi-sexual?" He sneered. "Just pick a side already."

His gun swung—a tiny pendulum—back and forth, resting at each peak as if deciding which way to point.

"You were there, Blue, leading, destroying my people, flying a flag of conquest." Green outlined the scene.

"Dude, that's weird. I experienced the exact same simulation as you, but in reverse. I led a bunch of sword-and-shield wusses—farmers, I think. Seriously, we couldn't hit a high rise if it grew right in front of our faces. Your people crossed our border, burned our land, and kept cutting us down, but I tried to reach you, tried to surrender in order to talk peace. I ordered them to form up and get to you no matter the cost. I even flew the white flag, but you kept shooting us with arrows and running away."

Green scoffed. "We attacked you?" *Click*.

"Yes. Why is that so hard to believe?"

"And you wanted peace? Why would you want peace? If someone attacked your people, fight back. Otherwise, you are weak. One more reason I should survive this contest."

"Well, yeah, in the real world, I suppose, but not in a simulation. Why would I want to kill you in a sim? I gain nothing and lose a partner who's going to help get us all out of here." Why did Green find collaboration so hard to understand?

"Because you want to survive in the real world, and I have tough news for you. You must accept that there is only one way to achieve that goal: outlive me."

"Yes, I want to live, but I don't want to kill. The hologram only controlled the setting; it didn't control me. I don't care about ancient history. I care about today. We have to get out of here, today."

"There is no way out. We've tried everything. Climbing ..." *click*, "digging ...", *click*, "stacking furniture. Prayer. Nothing works."

A frustrated Blue clenched his fist and punched the air. He hated the idea of giving up but conceded the point; they were out of ideas. One more reason to convince Green to focus on solutions, not on the problem.

From his bed across the room, the messenger of tough news arose and sauntered toward Blue, who laid his hand on his pistol resting on the stone floor. Green matched his casual, seated posture and set down his weapon, a peaceful parley through metal trees. His finger emphasized his points as he spoke.

"You know, I owned a successful business. Yeah, financial services. Big money. See the shirt? Eton brand. Where'd you get yours? Matalan?"

"I don't know what that means."

"What's the US equivalent?" Green looked down and snapped his fingers. "Ah, Target. Your wardrobe could use an upgrade."

Blue looked at his stained and ripped shirt. Had he left the tag hanging out?

Green continued, "I helped many companies from across the Middle East access the major western stock markets."

"That's great. Maybe when we escape, we go into business together."

Green smirked. "I modernized my country. Made us more like you, more western, like you said you wanted. Then you know what happened? A western company opened an office in my city with the same services. I watched as month after month they launched new stock offerings, while my business withered. 'Missing' paperwork, 'incorrect' risk calculations. Finally, I realized that invading company knew people at the exchanges and purposely blocked me, drove me out. Now,"—he wagged that finger—"now you want to work together, combine your superb marketing skills with my local knowledge?"

"Sure, why not?" It wasn't the worst idea ever.

Green shifted to a kneeling position, tucked his firearm safely away, and leaned closer.

"Why not? Because I could not fight a single foreign company, and I certainly cannot fight an alien planet. One way or another, only one of us is climbing that ladder in the middle to start a new business." He stood and glanced at Red, still hidden behind her desk bunker, maybe listening, maybe not. "Who knows? Maybe none of us will."

As Green strutted away, Blue called out. "Rasheed. The guys who hurt your business wore shirts like yours." Green never turned back. Pompous jerk.

As he rose and plodded to his own makeshift redoubt, an exhausted Blue suffered his last bit of hope deflating. The anguish of failing to collaborate made him scowl. He thrashed his arms through the air, silent-stomped the ground, and bit his fist instead of screaming. His creative energy was spent. He envisioned no path out of this hellhole.

Before plopping into bed, he pondered the lamp on his nightstand. It felt sturdy and housed conducting wires running up the middle. He finger-nail-tapped the broad base and shaft. It rang like metal. Using an outstretched hand to measure that base, he surreptitiously compared it to the space between the prison bars. The lamp was wider.

Perhaps it was time for a new plan.

13

Red's Vision.
Green's Fire

R ED WOKE TO A peaceful alarm of chirping birds, morning songs inviting
all to soak in a deep breath of fresh air and greet the life-giving sun as it
sauntered over the eastern hillside and bathed her bare arms. Blades of tall, soft
grass and fragrant wildflowers still shaded her eyes, easing her into a new day.
This was not the chamber.

Enjoying the pleasant reprieve, she sat up, head peering over the swaying
grains and low bushes of a lovely meadow next to a babbling brook. A casual
native outfit replaced her jeans and t-shirt. The skirt, though, hung shorter
than any she'd seen at rez festivals, barely covering her knees. She rubbed the
material, judged it to be modern, and detected plastic buttons. Tasseled leather
boots adorned her feet. Her camp nestled in a stand of fruit trees that offered
a tantalizing array of breakfast options—that first crack of biting into a crisp
apple. The concealment from those trunks also tempted in another way.

"Oh, I know it's just a sim, but for once I want to at least pretend like I can use the bathroom in privacy."

After retying her breechcloth and brushing off her skirt, she meandered upstream toward a village, content smile and her low hum setting the pace. Dozens of wooden roofs etched "welcome" across the horizon. The market along main street recently awoke as well. Shop doors swung open. Retailers set up their stalls. Smiling men and women greeted each other and guided fantastic beasts pulling carts filled with fresh fruits, fishes, plus fairy spices that smelled like half-cinnamon, half-lavender, and all joy. *That bipedal, bull-like creature looks familiar, like a peaceful, domesticated minotaur.* He lumbered forward, horned head swaying to an unheard melody while thick muscles flexed from his labors. It looked more like having fun than working.

She got why Blue enjoyed his sim so much. The detail amazed her, immersed her in the scene.

A dozen playful children in leather moccasins and colorful cotton shirts ran around a large table, throwing tiny fireballs and lightning bolts at each other while their male teacher scolded them to sit

She gasped. "Dad?" So many thoughts she regretted never sharing with him.

He stood behind one girl, finally seated on the bench but still bouncy, and leaned over her shoulder, one arm planted on the table, the other hand patting the student's back, praising her spelling. Red envisioned her own younger reflection in the faces at the table. This place came across as so familiar, so comfortable, so ... lifelike.

Whizz ... boom. A long hiss and an explosion ended the idyllic scene, first freezing it in a moment of processing the sudden change, then flinging it into a frenzied mess. The fireball from the sky burst outside the settlement, taking out a traveling cart or two. The next ones would surely strike closer to the heart of the peaceful hamlet.

She shuddered in fright, feet frozen on main street, unsure of how to react. Flashes from every major life decision—or indecision in her case—flooded back, but this time, she didn't have months to think about it.

Dotting the western sky much closer than the horizon chugged two short trains steaming ahead at attack speed. Deep purple engines shimmered in the early light. Dark, wispy clouds streaked the blue sky in the background. Planted on top, propped against the vertical exhaust chimney, pilots rode their mechanical monsters bareback into the fray. Frantically, they pointed one hand then the next back to the ethereal rails no longer needed behind the flying train, grabbed them with their minds, and willed them to the front, placing and connecting them to the advancing ones in whichever direction they desired to steer. No more than a couple of unused rails floated behind, and no more than a few protruded in front. Other than that magic, nothing held up these metal monsters. It was inhuman how aggressively the pilots worked, arms just a blur. White hair two-meter-long flapped in the wind behind them.

Sky Raiders!

Another fireball spat from the front hole of one machine, hurling toward the western houses. They splintered into thousands of burning embers, scorching the clothes of those scrambling out of the blast radius. The heatwave washed over her, singeing her eyes like she'd stared too long at a roaring campfire.

When the flying squad drew closer, archers popped over the sides of the trailing train cars like festering tumors, strafing the town with malignant volleys, pinning mothers to the blood-soaked ground.

One arrow sunk into the road between Red's feet, pinning a half-inhaled breath inside her throat.

As they passed overhead, she glimpsed the conductors hanging off the back of the locomotives, sadistic pleasure in their commands and cackles. One was Blue; the other was Green. Long tails of ornate, purple coats fluttered behind. Another villain shoveled evil fuel into the machine's ravenous furnace from the second car.

In the reprieve from their passing, before they turned to strike again, she shook herself, forced the wheels of her mind to churn and assess the damage, thoughts slipping as they gripped for any traction. Turn and flee? Duck into a building? All options wavered between promising and fatal.

Close by on the charred ground, one of those familiar-looking work beasts lay in agony, corded muscles heaving under quaking breath. For simple farmers, this creature was their livelihood. Helping him would help them. She dashed and kneeled beside him, placing a calming hand on his chest, each rise and fall a little shallower until the struggle ceased, a scent of fields and farm work all that remained to prove he had lived. She had arrived too late.

"I recognize you now. You are my creation. This village ... this is my novel from my mind."

Along the eastern horizon, two trains completed their wide turn and lined up for another deadly pass.

"Blue AND Green are the Pinta Machina King. I never realized he was a twin, but that makes sense for his backstory." She knew the King's cruelty all too well—he was her character. Now Blue and Green's cultures magnified it.

Desolation loomed for the village. Indecision morphed into dread.

From the web of alleyways surrounding the town square, a dozen Aprenti, those brave women warriors of the woods that she invented, took up firing positions, some covered by the corner of houses, some on their knees behind troughs. They lined up their fine-grained hardwood bows, ready to defend the innocent, ready to light up the sky. None shouldered a quiver—no need. As each powerful arm pulled on taut strings, mystical ether provided the arrow, forming one from potent tip to the end of the draw, gold lightning bolts with wisps of white energy swirling around the shaft. Let fly your righteous fury.

Shot after shot honed in on its target, gold explosions pockmarking the air around the lead train, but none slowed the ironed dragons.

One more fireball scattered or killed the last defenders.

Blue and Green slaughtered Red's creation. Dread flamed into burning rage.

As the two trains steamed toward another sweeping turn, a third spot appeared in the sky on an intercept course, at first too far away to identify. When the Sky Raiders lined up their next bombardment, the latecomer gained ground, a massive, grayish creature propelled with powerful, red dragon wings controlled by a lone rider. Each flap thundered across the meadow.

A Gray Dire!

A top-tier spirit animal an Aprenti can summon once in her lifetime, she caught one raider from behind, snatched the pilot from his perch then dropped the body like a bomb, a fine red mist rising from the impact. With nobody to haul magic rails from behind to the front, the train outran the track and plummeted to a fiery demise, blasting up the soil and spreading its flaming fuel and mangled fighters across main street a few shops in front of her. Chunks of dirt pelted her and shattered nearby windows.

Witnessing the tide turn in favor of her people brought a buzz, a throng of pride that amped up her already thumping chest. While watching in awe, raging heart emboldened by the revenge, victorious fist pumping the air, a tiny hand tugged on her shirttail. She turned to find a pre-teen village girl with a message.

"The Apprentice say, don't trust duplicitous Blue. We have delivered him into your hands. End your enemy's reign of terror today."

Red checked the progress of the air battle, silently mouthing, "*Apprentice?*"

Death and destruction all around, and now a grammar error threw salt in her metaphorical paper cut right when her people were winning. "First of all, apprentice is singular, so use the right verb. Secondly,"—flipping back to the courier, she asked to clarify—"who is the ..." but the child had vanished into the swirling chaos of the crowd. "OK, so you won't tell me what you meant by Blue, either."

The second Sky Raider no longer maintained air superiority and retreated to the scum pit it called home.

The Gray Dire, that victorious calvary, encircled the smoldering village before landing on the main strip next to her destroyed trophy.

Her controlling pilot hopped off and sauntered about like a site-seeing tourist, dressed in a wool vest adorned with rows of colorful beads and geometric shapes, cotton headband wrapped around his forehead with a single, large feather sticking out the back, the distinctive air of a non-First Nations tribesman, a tribes-*man*, who copied style from the black-and-white movie rerun app.

She did a double take. *Blue?!? Triplets?*

The audacity. If firepower couldn't wipe out her people, the oppressor could just appropriate her culture, water it down until no flavor remained. A man co-opted her for-women-only Gray Dire, her for-indigenous-only clothing, and probably wanted her to thank him. Not today.

Red unsheathed her flint dagger, confusion clouding an already rabid mind. Rage tunneled her vision directly to the Pinta Machina tyrant. She dashed the short distance toward him.

"Oh, hey, Willa. What's up? Slaps for the dragon grizzly, am I right?"

With a war cry, she leaped in the air and aimed leather-booted feet at his face, planting them instead in his gut, dropping on her side after her flying kick. The attacker-savior reeled, landing on the ground hunched over, heaving, gulping for air that would not comply.

She recovered from her fall. All around lay slivered boards, smoking beams, and still bodies. "Look what you and Green did to my village, to my world."

On his knees, he still couldn't breathe, much less mount a defense, wheezing while holding up a hand of surrender and pointing to himself with the other.

She skirted his side, clamping an arm around his forehead while she kneeled behind, business edge of her blade pressed against his throat. Weeping blurred her sight; chest quivered as she released her grief. Eyes strained, pressed tight then relaxed, repeatedly, like never-satisfied pumps drawing tears from a deep, emotional cistern seething with anger and loss, hate and unfulfilled hopes. Blue-Pinta slapped her arm, wiggled his body, struggled to escape. Her mind wavered between reality and simulation, undulated between high conscious knowledge and low primal emotion. Which was true?

"No, no, no. You stole too much from me already. You won't get away with it, not here, not today, not when I am unfettered to stop you." With a silent determination, she slid that blade across his useless throat, unshackled her grip on him as he loosened his grip on life, and let the body flop face first to the dust.

Justice delivered, but the smoldering consequences of the crime still filled her nostrils, unhealed.

It was just a sim, after all.

She shifted from kneeling to sitting, crossed her legs, and dropped a wet face into her hands, pouring out the last remains of anger. More flowed than she expected, more than what a holographic head game should evoke. This well must have been dug deeper and further in the past than she realized. As she emerged from her ocean of pain and reached the safe shores of dry eyes, she drowned in a flood of shame for stooping so low, for acting like she promised herself she never would, for responding with violence like "them"—like a savage.

So much for holiday oaths among drinking buddies on the reservation. So much for a better world in a future when she's in charge.

"Ow." Blue coughed and choked as he roused, blowing tiny dust billows around his face.

No! She scooted backwards, dagger aimed forward. *Just die already.* Would this now turn into a horror sim? Some loser male hunting her through dark woods to violently steal what he couldn't gain with charm?

"What the hell, Willa? You know you can't die in a simulation, right, but you still feel everything?" He rolled onto his back, scrawny chest straining, soaking in deep breaths, hands cupping his uninjured throat. "Wait. Technically, I don't know that's true. *You* don't know that's true. What if you really killed me?" He groaned while he sat up.

"Blue? Is that ... you? Or are you Pinta still screwing with me?"

"Who? No, it's me, the real me. Well, not real-real, you know, but it's me in your sim, yes."

Pinta Machina was eloquent, which meant Blue sat before her, flustered.

"Why would you kill me, Willa?"

With an unshakable quaver in her voice, she explained what she had become—out loud but more to herself. "I ... was furious. This place is more than real. To me, it's more alive than I am. How could I know for sure it was you? I didn't know it was you. I didn't know we could enter each other's visions. If I knew you were real, I wouldn't necessarily want you to die, but honestly, at that moment, I didn't care because of how seeing you destroy that village made me feel. Killing what you represent, though ... yeah, let's do it again."

"And what, exactly, do I represent, Willa?"

She glared at his fuzzy outline. "Are you being serious right now? Look around? See all this destruction? This is what both your culture and Green's do. His conquest just happened on the other side of the world, where I live now. So, I know that history like I know my own."

"Do you really, Willa? Do you know your own history? Are you telling me that your tribe never conquered another? Or that surrounding tribes never carried your ancestors into slavery? Or mine, for that matter?"

A heavy chest throbbed while a swirling head failed to focus. No stories to refute his accusation surfaced, but of course, her people were better than that, more enlightened. Stuff down the impulse to throw dirt in his face. She diverted for now until she could revisit the topic later, better prepared. "Besides, if you were ... you, you wouldn't actually die, not after an entire skyscraper fell on Green and he returned his typical, cheery self, right?"

"Fortunately, I guess, but let's not test the theory again, ok? Do you feel better now?"

She sat still until the trembling ceased. "Maybe? Maybe. At least now you've tasted the depth of pain in a single moment that I've experienced from a lifetime of oppression. And maybe it crossed my mind that it might be you, but I didn't think it through. I figured, if this was the alien's way of by-passing their stupid one-bullet dilemma, at least there would be fewer of you in the world to come—less of ... this poser crap." She waved a disgusted dagger at his outfit.

"You killed me over a costume?" Blue ripped off the feathered headband and flung it into a small fire flickering from the downed Sky Raider train. "Sorry," he chirped, "there wasn't time to research *authentic native* clothing trends." His head bobbed. "Besides, you never told me what tribe you're from, so I just picked something cool from the avatar options on the computer. Don't blame me; blame whoever built this world."

Not sure if that comment veiled an insult, she sat in silence, further calming her nerves, regaining her composure, assessing her rival. He, Gray Dire he, had, after all, defended her village from himself, the Sky Raider version of himself.

"I didn't kill *you*. In my mind, I killed that guy." She pointed to the burning train wreck. "I was mad. It was like punching you in the arm to relieve my stress, to express my feelings."

"Have you seen my arms? They can't take a punch."

Don't smirk. "What are you doing here, Blue?"

"Trying to help," he rose and kicked a clump of dirt generally toward her, "but now I'm pissed. After the BS shade they threw at me and Rasheed, I knew they'd hit you the same. Since his sim paralleled mine, I figured there was some kind of shared holo-space. So, I dug into the menus, saw a folder pop up when your bars turned into boulders, presumed that was your sim. I entered here as soon as I exited mine. I knew you could use a friend, that's all."

Blue seemed sincere as he stomped away to examine the crinkled iron wreckage. He tromped around the hot flares licking at his feet, kicked a large wheel or two, then dug around the fuel car behind the engine.

"Hey, Willa. It's a book with you pictured as the author. Whoa. They filled the entire train car with your books. Were these guys stealing them?"

Curious, the now level-headed warrior rose and stepped to his side. Indeed, the fuel Sky Raider Kings Green and Blue had shoveled into their death trains consisted only of copies of her future ground-breaking novel, cover art just as enticing as she imagined, author headshot just as distinguished yet whimsical as she pictured. The sales copy was all blurred, though. Of course, they wouldn't give any useful ideas. This was obviously one more metaphorical mind-screw envisioned by diabolical alien imaginations.

"Willa, what happened here?"

"You and Green attacked my village, killed my people, and apparently enjoyed burning books."

"I didn't do any of this; a manufactured evil, with my face photoshopped on it, did this. You're being manipulated. You know what's weird? Just like you heard me tell Rasheed, in my sim, you burned down my family's business and threw our favorite book in a fire, too."

She sneered.

"In fact, how much should we bet that Fake You is burning a sacred book in Rasheed's sim right now?" He offered to shake on it. When she ignored him long enough, he reached for her head. "You have dirt in your hair."

She recoiled, slapped his hand away, and brushed her own hair clean.

Sounds of recovery drifted from the village. She surveyed the survivors dousing fires, healing wounds, and buttressing houses. They were a resilient tribe, after all. One mental imprint emerged, forming amidst her wrecked emotions. She owed her best to those she represented, to her community of strangers. She ached for them to live, the real them out in the real world, and now knew she could do whatever it took to protect them. Hatred for the aliens grew because they forced her to care, forced her to want to win for her people.

In a makeshift school, a lone male teacher corralled children while parents dragged heavy loads of debris and the dead to a growing pyre. That selfless professor distracted some students with their familiar routine while drying the eyes of others with his handkerchief. *He found a way to sacrifice for his people too, didn't he?*

An image flashed of her and Dad hugging one last time, mixing emotions like a lapping wave churning up sand and foam. Her bare feet remained stuck in the refreshing water and grinding grit.

"I didn't do any of this, Willa." Blue strode to the schoolhouse, leveled a tilted table, and aligned the benches. He stood behind one child, seated but still weepy, and leaned over her shoulder, one skinny arm planted on the table, the other hand patting the student's back, praising her artistry.

She gravitated there, drawn by the return to normalcy amidst the wreckage.

The head pedagogue stepped to this new assistant and shook his hand in gratitude. Eye to eye, man to man, the two conversed, exchanged life's tidbits, and laughed. Dad accepted Blue's help.

The scene stuttered, then froze. Pixels blurred, then enlarged until each stretched into nothingness, giving way to the reality of a dank chamber once again. On the other side of the metal barrier, Blue stood, arm reaching out to her as if still enjoying a fatherly handshake.

Maybe it was time to help oppose her captors. Maybe she could ally with a historical rival against her current tormentors. Maybe it was time for a new plan.

"Hey, uh, Rasheed. Want to compare notes on our latest holo-sim?"

Blue shouting from the central ladder broke Red's contemplative silence while relaxing in bed. *Ugh, what now?*

Green didn't stir from his bed. "No. Go away."

"Uh, OK. Maybe later, but tell me one thing. Were there any, oh, I don't know, flames involved?" Blue's voice still crowed louder than necessary.

Green leaped from his bed and strode to the ladder. "Don't screw with me, Blue. I'm not in the mood."

Red sat up and leaned over the side of her protective desk. Blue messed with her, she knew it, and risked a fight with Green. No one should poke the bear.

Blue held up his hands and maintained his volume. "Sure thing, just answer this one question. It'll really help me understand our situation."

Green turned and walked away, scowling. "What?"

"In your most recent hologram vision, did anyone burn your favorite books?"

Green stopped abruptly and stood silent for a minute, just glaring at her.

She shriveled inside.

"Yes," was all he uttered before returning to bed, deadpan, laying with his face to the wall.

From the center of the chamber, Blue mouthed, "Told you," while gesturing for her to pay up.

She flashed him the zero symbol. *You'll get nothing from me.*

Blue pranced in silence, simultaneously raising a knee and opposing elbow, alternating sides. That douche bag co-opted a generic, American pop-culture rendition of native steps as his victory dance. She could almost hear the 'Heya Heya.' When done offending that way, he stooped, touched the ground with one straight index finger and rubbed his other against it, then mimicked blowing on the ground. *Ah, he's starting a fire. I get it.* Standing tall, he stuck out his chest, formed an O with his lips as if yawning, and quickly moved his open palm towards and away, back and forth. *War cry, yes, get it all out of your system.* Curling an arm as if holding a bag, he reached in and flung its invisible contents into the supposed fire. *Yeah, yeah, books. You made your point.*

She lay back down but raised two middle fingers above the desk wall that shielded her while she slept.

Damn Blue for being right, but at least it shed light on the diabolical visions. Damn the visitors. She would never burn another culture's writings. She loved books, but now she had to overcome Green's perception that she would based on nothing real.

More importantly, she realized she needed to erase any hateful ideas implanted by her own visions. Intellectually, she judged them fake, but emotions still broiled with each replay in her mind.

Ugh.

14

TYPO

"Switching to sim camera number four. Ready on one." Sudhira, Lead Studio Production Technician for the most popular hit show in her lifetime, Charlotte's OBD, worked the joysticks controlling the camera angles like the old pro she was. She'd watch the scene for enjoyment later. For now, it was just bits and pieces that needed concentrated stitching. One loss of focus could be the difference between an Emmy and a Razzie.

"I want a closeup on Red's face when the first fireball hits. Don't miss that money shot like when Blue hit Green with the arrow." Deandra, Live Television Director, barked orders to her professional staff as she chased two more Motrin with an energy drink. "Cue sentimental music, half volume. Scroll pictures of Red and her dad on the rez, sepia filter. Go to one, slow zoom, and ..."

Whizz ... boom. Many in the control room flinched when the simulated explosion shook the scene.

"... got it. Nice work, people. Perfect jitter, Sudhira. Looked like a real camera shaking, and that face frozen with fear is worth two-tenths in the ratings."

"Stand back everyone; boss-gal is on fire," Sudhira quipped from her station.

"You bet your momma's shoes I am. Now stop kissing my butt and prep that scene with the magic pilots making the trains fly. Then get back to kissing my butt. That's why you're my favorite, Sudhira. The rest of you could learn a lesson." Deandra and her room full of dance partners continued the tango between the script leading on one screen and Red's spontaneous reactions to the simulation on the others, knowing what surprise moves lurked and wowing the audience with each effortless sequence.

"Go to the wide angle with the flying trains turning to strike again. Now get me those closeups of fake Blue and Green cackling. Switch to b-roll of Red day-dreaming about this novel. Pan to the pen and blank paper on her nightstand. Sad, really, when you think about it. This entire creative world locked up in her head because she's too inhibited to release it. Remember that, people. Art dies in fear."

"Uh, Dee, we have a problem. Blue's flying into the sim." Sudhira never took eyes off the screen.

"Uh, yeah. He's in train two. What's the problem?"

"No, I mean real Blue. He entered the sim space on a flying grizzly bear. That's not in the script."

"How's that possible?"

"You're asking me? How do a handful of alien ships fly across the galaxy and hold half-a-planet hostage? I don't question much these days. In training, the Network mentioned it was possible because the room shares subroutines, but they didn't plan this."

"Let it play. It'll add a delicious dash of drama and a tantalizing touch of tension. Doesn't change our job. Make people watch; get paid; stay alive. Fly sim drone camera one behind the grizzly in case he does something memorable. Do we have extracted memories with Blue scared of heights, or crashing a drone, a kite, anything?"

Deandra's phone rang. "It's Cy," she said. He was the Producer and Network Liaison, her boss. She had to answer. He rarely called, but when he did, Deandra's personality stiffened.

"Yeah, we see him. Advice? … Okay, hold one. Send it directly to Sudhira." She pulled the phone to her chest and barked an order, "Sudhira, get me a villager, someone Red would believe and care about—a local prepubescent female. Tear-stained face for sympathy, but no crying; Red finds that pathetic. Cy's pinging you a message to deliver … verbatim."

Sudhira eyed Cy's message in her chat client: The Apprentice say, don't trust duplicitous Blue … She instinctively began correcting the typo, but then froze. In its rush, The Network meant to type 'Aprenti,' Red's imagined brave women warriors of the woods. Perhaps auto-correct just delivered this closet resistance member the opportunity she longed for—any way to deliver a message of hope to the unwitting players in an alien psychological drama, any way to let them know they were not alone. Red would certainly recognize the incongruence, and it would break her out of the trance of that hyper-realistic, hypnotic simulation. Sudhira had no clue why the occupiers spent so much energy broadcasting these rooms, but she knew the rooms represented their greatest strength: demoralizing us, separating us, focusing us on hating our differences rather than fighting our common tyrants.

Dee said verbatim.

Following direct instructions from her boss never stung before. Her fingers tingled, and she eyed the room for spies before committing the seditious act of obedience. She scanned the NPCs—non-player characters, everyone in the sim besides Red and real Blue—and selected the closest to Red that met the criteria. A few accurate keystrokes reprogrammed the courier away from crying in absolute terror to hustling on a mission, mock wind drying sham tears along the way. The pre-teen villager arrived and tugged on Red's shirt tail.

Message delivered. Maybe it helped.

"Hey, Dee. At least real Blue showing up saved Red from watching fake Blue kill her fake dad," Sudhira observed. "Say that three times real fast."

"Hm. We came out ahead in the ratings, sure, but I would have taken both."

The rest of the drama played out: tears, conflict, a death and resurrection ending with catharsis, forgiveness, and perhaps an inkling of cooperation. Deandra made the magic. The production crew executed with precision and professionalism. Now, she just had to wait for the ratings, and for the blackout hood over her head.

The control room was more than a studio. It was a major military asset for the occupiers. Thus, they kept its location secret with a routine enforced with a rigor Sudhira hated. After rough guards prodded the crew into a van, forced on a hood and headset to muffle road sounds, they drove a random route that always took thirty minutes regardless of which turns followed which stops. Finally, they deposited her a few blocks from home.

The evening stroll wound past street shops manned by unsmiling vendors lingering until the clock flashed quitting time. She inserted her Bluetooth earbuds before stopping at the flower stand, gazing at the meager options, the day's buzz still surfing her skin.

"Looking for a special occasion?" This female clerk cracked a faint smile.

"Yeah, I want to send that …" She clenched her eyes while remembering the exact code phrase. "… that *specific* kind of message to that *certain* kind of person. You know what I mean?"

The clerk raised her eyebrows. "I have exactly what you need, yes. Try these." She handed Sudhira a premade bouquet and took payment of five times the going rate. "Return the vase for your deposit back."

Sudhira sauntered down the block waiting for her headset to pair with the burner phone hidden in the arrangement, whistling the first notes of an un-formed song. Once the confirmation beeped, she 'sniffed' the flowers to speak.

"Noor Inayat-Khan, reporting a significant development." A sweet code-name; it both honored her heritage and fit the current times.

"Glad to hear you're still around, Noor. State your report."

"Hey, Sarge. Did you catch the local one-bullet dilemma room today? Notice anything out of the ordinary?"

"What in that poop show is ever ordinary? Trains don't fly and grizzlies don't grow dragon wings."

"Yeah, yeah, that's just the fantasy backdrop to the real story, the deeply personal psychological basis for the tension, but forget that. Did you catch the anomaly?"

"You mean the typo in the little girl's message? Was that you?"

"I don't want to brag, no need for a medal, but uh, yeah. The opportunity just fell into my lap. I'm glad I recognized it before it was too late. I don't know; I hope it pulled her from the psycho-trauma a little bit. Maybe now she knows she has friends on the outside. Maybe it pointed out it's the aliens who want her to hate Blue and Green, and who would burn her books."

"Good work, Noor. We'll take wins when we can, especially if we walk away to fight another day. Working on a new mission for you. Deets at our next meeting."

"Hey, Sarge. When are we dropping the online stuff and meeting in person? I need a brilliant smile to go with that soothing voice." He better be blushing right now.

"Unfortunately, not until the first battle. Don't worry, Noor. It'll arrive soon enough."

15

TRAILHEADS

R ED TOSSED AND TURNED. Sleep hid from her in the shadows. Maybe someone screwed with the temperature tonight. Or maybe occasional tinkering noises glided across the stone from the darkness in Blue's direction.

The insomniac stealthily slid the covers down and slipped away from the safety of her desk-fortified bed, bare feet fuming at the floor's icy touch. Curiosity shut them up and force-marched them quietly toward the noise, a trail of chills. She only dared twenty silent steps without knowing for sure where that electric fence waited to ambush her from the abyss.

After adjusting to the umbra, the irregularly scheduled lights-out setting, eagle eyes barely discerned Blue's shadowy outline kneeling on the floor next to his bed. He held the ghost of his table lamp, minus the shade, at an angle to the floor, grinding it back and forth, gently, smoothly. Keen ears, though, detected the lightest scratch each time.

A few minutes later, the shady one placed the lamp on the floor and slithered behind the protective desktop on his bed, both his shadow and intent merging behind a shield of secrecy.

Calling on the spirit of a cat, she slinked back to bed, curiosity unsatisfied. In fact, her mind raced more than before. She did not sleep that night.

Red stood still except for a tapping foot and jittery fingers at the end of crossed arms. She couldn't relax and enjoy the sweeping view of grasslands and hillsides. Instead, she questioned her decision to come here today, judged it as too impulsive, but also hoped to break the stalemate in her chamber.

Now that the prisoners enjoyed occasional access to the simulations—the holo-deck, as the resident nerd called it—the three spent more time there than in reality. The wardens allowed very limited settings, all meant to provoke conflict and stress the players' psyche. So, walk fifteen-second laps around a cramped prison cave pointing a gun at the only two humans she knew for sure were alive, or suffer psychological torture that induced a deeper desire to kill those same two men, but at least where fake sunshine warmed her arms. Two horrible choices, but Red was too intrigued to pass on Blue's promise that he'd found a work-around, a loophole. His invite to a friendly, conflict-free hike presented a perfect opportunity to delve a little deeper into this guy's credibility.

"Hey, Willa. Thanks for joining me. You look nice."

Oh crap! She never thought about what to wear, and just clicked default "casual, easy hike, cool and sunny day, with Blue" for her apparel. After he turned his back to head toward the trailhead, her glance found a comfortable, forest-green, cotton mini-skirt covering black spandex tights and a black sports bra topped with a loose-fitting, matching cotton tank propelled by ankle-high hiking boots. A tied-off, light fleece jacket accented her waist. Cute enough to stay sane for a day.

His casual outfit looked fine, too. Thin legs poked from olive green, nylon hiking shorts, yet his calves flexed with each step, revealing chiseled definition. A blue, tight-fitting, moisture-wicking top completed the ensemble. Neat, co-ordinated, and respectable. Each strapped a water bottle to their hip.

He paused at the fork. "What do you think? Up a hill or along a river?"

Up promised magnificent views across the valley. The river, though, drew her along its shores with a peaceful melody. Hills meant climbing, more effort. River meant waist-high crossings, wet and chilly.

"I don't know. You decide."

"Up it is then."

The blue sky shepherded puffy white clouds in a slow-motion trek across the surrounding horizons. Beautiful green and brown mountains colored the right side. On the left, across a crystal-clear rocky stream, a field flourished with tall grasses and vibrant wildflowers, their fragrance drifting by on the balmy breeze, occasional fairies popping above the blades to chase butterflies and kiss the petals, releasing a magical mini firework show that crackled in the air and sprinkled spices on the ground.

This was her world, the land of the Aprenti, from the first holographic hate-fest foisted upon her.

"Interesting choice, Blue. Why hike here?"

"Are you kidding? This place is fantastic. I don't know who created it, but they're a genius. Native kids running around blasting each other in the butt with green lightning bolts? Dragon grizzlies? That's gold right there. I only wish I was half as creative."

She did not detect any BS, but this was the guy who spent nights doing secret stuff, a guy under as much evolutionary pressure as she was to survive a sadistic game of galactic tyrants.

"What do you like about this place?" she asked.

"Everything. First of all, thinking up the idea shows brain power I'll never possess, but then I realized I have ideas, too, some good, others not so much. But I don't pursue my good ideas. Guess I'm too lazy, or not talented. Whoever filled out this world, though, is not only smart but also diligent enough to follow through. I wish I had people like that in my life. Maybe it would rub off."

Do you really, even if those people are like me? "It's not all fairies and magic; there's conflict, too. You saw the Sky Raiders, what they do."

"Yeah, in this world you will have troubles. There's no avoiding that, but it's what you do in response to conflict, how you handle it, that matters." He paused for a breath and offered her a refreshing sip. "It's who you partner with to get through the rough times in life that matters."

"They built this sim around the village. What made you explore the outskirts?"

"Nothing else I've tried worked. My well of ideas was exhausted. I stared at the problem for hours, walking around my room, slapping walls, staring into my toilet, looking at the ladder, analyzing these sims, approaching it head-on. I'm at the Hail Mary point now. Time to look outside the box and flip this problem on its head, you know?"

The hike continued, winding through slowly-rising, tree-shaded hillsides. That pinch of pine scent permeated the air. A dependable grip steadied her over a stretch of boulders. Trusty arms holding her waist softened her hop off a fallen tree. A secure hand, pressed against her lower back, braced her up a steep incline. Honest smiles sprung from her jokes. Honest questions probed her master's thesis. Fallen sticks cracked beneath their feet. Buzzing bugs nipped at their necks. Sunshine warmed her face; conversation thawed her heart.

As they perched on a jutting overlook, snacking on berries bursting with flavor and peering across a valley a hundred meters down, the world seemed normal, at peace—except for dots circling a familiar village skyline already smoking from the Sky Raiders' distant attack. The vile scenario played out whether the two pugilists stepped into the ring to fight or sat viewing from the balcony. It was as if the programmers knew no other storyline besides destruction.

"Shouldn't we go help?" Conflicted, bemoaning the death of her people but enlivened by the moment, she flinched at each new billow of dust from another fireball.

"Sure, if you want. I call the Dragon Grizzly, er, sorry, the Gray Dire." He smirked. "Who gave you naming rights, by the way? Dragon Grizzly is way cooler."

She punched his arm.

"But seriously, Willa. Why bother with the Sky Raiders? It's a fake narrative meant to rile us up, pit us against each other rather than focus on solutions to our real dilemma."

"So, what's your proposal?"

He stared across the expanse, either contemplative or building suspense like his typical melodramatic self, but failed to deliver. He hung his head and shook it. "I don't know, Willa. I just don't know. Every idea is either bat guano crazy or ... I don't enjoy thinking about it."

"What does Green say?"

"He's one of those problems I don't want to think about. No matter what I try, what I say, he's always angry at me. You handle him better than I do. You're more level-headed."

She never noticed before that his voice rang deep, matured, not pip-squeaky like she would have imagined in her head based on his svelte frame. She reached out to rub his shoulder.

He turned her way, head still hung. "All I know is you're the competent one. I want to work with you, not against you. If our other roomie won't help ..."

His words hung in the air like a vapor bridge, closing the gap between them, fogging and blurring as his body faded on the other side.

"Looks like my meter expired. This was nice, Willa. Next time, you pick the trail. See you soon."

After he disappeared, his memory lingered. What a charming day. She lay back against the stony outcrop, thoughts drifting to the swirling eagle overhead. This world was genius, but would Mark feel the same if he learned it formed in her mind's eye? Would he still support her dream, or secretly plan to destroy it, at night, in the dark, scraping a lamp against the floor? How do you flip this dilemma on its head?

After the gentle blue sky succumbed to a murky cave ceiling, she sat up in bed and folded her arms across the desk, leaning over the side of that protective wall and peering across two rooms to Blue who also sat on the edge of his bed watching her and smiling.

I wonder what he's thinking about?

16

Persistent Bits

Rafiq tucked his little girl into bed and told his best lady good night before cracking open test equipment on the dining room table. He'd collected a few days' worth of readings from the OBD data feed, and it was time to test his theory.

Sipping herbal tea from his istikan, an Iraqi tea cup, he time-stamped the holographic simulations from the OBD to correlate with the data stream. His presumption was that the data fed those simulations. Characterizing the stream could lead to a way to track the source. Maybe network addresses were embedded unencrypted. That would be nice.

"Wow." Turns out he had wasted time. He should have looked at the stream first, because it never ended. Maybe certain frequencies shifted, some arose only during the sims, others came and went randomly, but a vast amount of data always flowed, regardless.

He had to let Sarge know, so he texted, "Hey, remember that data stream I told you about? Turns OUT it's always turned ON. That was a terrible pun. I'll work on it."

Sarge replied, "What does that mean?"

"Means I can write a better punchline."

"No, about the data stream always on."

"Oh, yeah, of course. Uh, I don't know. I have a theory, but it's crazy. I'll get back to you."

"OK. Thanks for the intel. Keep at it and bring it to our next meeting."

17

The Final Spark

L IKE STARING AT THE blank first page of the next influential novel, Red knew the goal but couldn't see the plan, couldn't form the words. Unfortunately, Blue's constant prodding failed to spur her imagination to run wild; it just beat the dead horse.

"Come on, what are we not thinking about? There has to be a way out."

The three death row inmates, armed, stood close to the central circular fence surrounding that ladder, staring at the unseen top, the promised pardon to the lone survivor. Rolling a chair against the iron blooms confirmed they still sizzled. The sheet tied to the back reeled it in for the next day's attempt, another scorch mark to track the countdown.

"By the way, great idea with the chair, Willa." Blue complemented her ingenuity, a soothing contrast to interactions with most males who would have felt threatened. She had told her brother which direction was North, and if he hadn't been high, he may have agreed. That night in the woods alone didn't hurt him, but it didn't help their relationship, either. Somehow, he blamed her. Maybe she'd see him again someday and laugh about it.

"Maybe we can dance our way out." She threw a verbal jab at Blue who blocked with a poor rendition of the easy ceremonial dance she recently taught him. Awkward, like moonwalking on carpet in cleats. She snickered at the goof. It was cute he tried, at least.

"If you two are through joking around ..." Green tossed a wet blanket on the silliness, dousing the spark of fun, one of the few fleeting moments of levity in an otherwise dismal existence.

She retorted, "Just having a quick laugh, Green. Otherwise, we'd cry." Cry like at her dad's funeral when she wanted to laugh at the memory of one of his classic jokes.

Blue continued to force five steps into the three-step jig. "What—my def moves don't bring a tear of joy to your eyes?"

Green minced no words. "No, Blue, they don't, and they don't inspire any new ideas, either. You're the 'big idea' man, and every one so far a colossal failure. We should discuss how we end this trial—discuss who should survive."

Blue transitioned into serious mode, rhythm of feet morphing into fidgeting, artistic sweeping of hands transforming into tapping his gun against his leg.

All emotionally drained jailbreakers bore their sole weapon at their side, ready for the end should this be the last meal. With tensions amping, any spark could trigger the final showdown.

"At least I'm trying to save us. All your calculations are about which of our deaths brings you the most satisfaction. Hint—neither will." Magnified motions escorted each of Blue's phrases.

True.

Green threw both hands in the air, then rolled up a sleeve to remind his roommates about the wrist-to-elbow burn mark, undeniable proof of dedication to the team—at least occasionally. "I wrapped pillows around my arms and tried to climb an electrified fence for one of your ideas, Blue. Did that succeed?" *Sniff.* "It still smells like, I don't know, charcoal."

True.

Blue started to bellow, then backed down the volume. "At least ... sorry, Willa. I'm trying not to yell because I remember that upsets you. At least we tried something productive, and you made it further than you predicted."

That comment launched Green into motion. He paced the length of his bars, rambling to no one in particular as he summarized options over and over, voice fading as he withdrew, then gaining clarity on the return trip. "I kill Red; Blue kills me; Blue wins. Can't have that. Either Blue or Red kill me, the other dies next. No. Think. Think. How do you get both? Choke one, shoot the other? Falling rock?"

"Come on, Rasheed. Don't give up now. We're past the hard part. We survived the simulations without killing each other. Now we're gelling, working together, right? Back me up here, Mark." She could count on his cooperation. It was his favorite mantra, after all.

Blue dropped his head and slumped his shoulders as if resigned to a dismal verdict. "Don't worry. I got your back." But actions contradicted the glum words. He ran a free hand through unkempt hair—squeezing a clump—bounced the gun on his temple, and turned his back. He stepped to his bed, moved the lamp from its perfectly fine hiding spot to an arm's length away, toward the tension, then fiddled with the sheets and fluffed his pillows.

Did he just crack? Am I all alone here, the only sane one left?

Green shortened his laps and increased the pace, only quick-stepping four times before the turn, then three, before settling into a two-stride routine and shorter sentences. He brandished his pistol, rapped his forehead with it, muttering like a madman losing grip on reality, mental stability swirling down a drain of despair. Disheveled hair and tense cheeks told the harrowing story from the past weeks. The stale punch of male musk hung in the air.

Each frenzied circuit raised her temperature. Both hands clenched the gun low by her waist, finger on then off the trigger, stiff arms primed to rise and level those sights instantly. She wavered on her feet, shifting weight left and right, and wondered why her backup continued to stay distant.

"Mark, we need you! I don't know what to do. Green's losing it."

He remained aloof, coldhearted, watching with a solemn stare, not helping, empty hands shaking at his sides, feet bouncing like warm-up steps of a jogger waiting for the light to change at an intersection.

She stood and pleaded—alone. "Please, Green, Rasheed, can we settle for a minute, just sit and talk a little longer?"

Green finally triggered, dashed toward her with a new venom, and thundered, "No, enough talk. I will defeat you both."

Her arms sprung up, aiming at the aggression, begging it to back down.

"Shoot me, Red! Go ahead, you know this helpless dog over there is waiting so he can end your miserable life. Go ahead, fall for his plan. He's played you all along."

Had he?

She pivoted, training her sights on the steely schemer still warming up his calves, unarmed, sticking close to his bed and that lone, shade-less, bulb-less lamp on the floor.

Blue presented no physical threat, but his menacing mental state distracted, disoriented her.

From her periphery, she eyed the existential peril.

Green raised his gun at her. *Damn, Mark. Because of you, he got the drop on me.*

She aimed back, barrel of her firearm fluttering all about his fuzzy center mass, her last inhale blocked halfway, now stuck in her throat—a breathless standoff.

Green stood just beyond the prison bars between his room and Blue's, cold steel aimed only at her.

Blue must have channeled the spirit of a cheetah. With no warning, she only caught the final streak of his attack.

He raced forward into the deadly, electrified bars, metal lamp aimed ahead like a spear, thrusting the base with a pillow insulating his hands. The point slid between two rods, unshocked, and punctured Green's rib below the armpit, exposed by raising his gun. His anger made the difference, opened the path for his demise. Once the lamp base smashed into the billets, closing the circuit, loud sparks crackled, drowning out his scream.

The white-hot bolts blinded her, stumbled her back, hands flung high and head swiveled low to shade her eyes. Through protective arms, she watched the vibrating glow, a spectacular and horrible light show just beyond.

Green's shadow stiffened while immense power danced about.

When the final spark flew, all was silent.

She lowered shivering arms, eyes readjusted to normalcy.

The murderer stood shriveled, shaking, eyes wide, arms still protecting a whitened face, pillow dropped to the floor. He skittishly reached for the electric fence, hand inching ever closer between each recoil, until he tapped a spark-free rod; the dead circuit hummed no more, leaving behind an iron skeleton.

The victim stood tall and frozen, eyes also wide, arms stiff and stretched to each side, gun still grasped, stuck lamp still protruding from his side, heavy base lying on the chest-high metal crossbeam. No blood flowed; no skin sizzled; no clothing smoked.

What just happened? She shut down. Her mind stalled, unable to crank out a thought or a twitch. Before the serene scene shifted a single frame, it faded to black. The lamp crumbled, withered, and disintegrated into fine dust that disappeared before soiling the bitter ground, a replay of every simulation shutdown sequence she had previously witnessed. Next vanished two more lamps, three desks, one by one, soiled sheets and flat pillows, all beds, and the rest of the spartan furnishings. Nothing remained but bleak walls. The few meager possessions they clung to these past weeks, complained about, used for security—all fake. In reality, they only had each other and their prison bars the entire time—and their guns.

Green, ashen faced, patted his body and checked the wound. He looked as stunned as she felt. Lifting his shirt to reveal an unpierced side, he turned to Blue but uttered no condemnation.

Her eyes followed, landing on a wilted man who dared to act single-handedly after incessant hours advocating for teamwork, for everyone surviving, for rational cooperation. These past few moments of truth revealed all her history with him as a lie. Betrayal. If he was capable of that act of unprovoked violence, what would he do to her—when she walked into his room while he's hanging out with friends; when she accidently stepped on his game controller; or any of a dozen other innocent sibling violations?

A little bile burned her throat. She hustled to her toilet, now vanished; nothing remained but an actual hole filled with vile stool. An overwhelming fetor punched her face. She dropped to her knees and retched with nobody to hold back her long hair and mangled feathers.

Before the nausea passed, all light disappeared. Nothing remained but blackness and hints of feet scurrying across nearby floors. She slapped the surroundings until she found her gun, rolled until seated, and shuffled backward until pressed against the stone boundary. Her sleeve soaked up the remaining saliva dripping from her chin, but her stomach still convulsed. She sat exposed now, nowhere to hide once the revealing lights returned.

How could you leave me in the dark about your plans, Mark?

After a few minutes of labored breathing, Green's accent lighting blinked, that green outline tracing the limits of his pen, publicizing his position. Once stygian again, she heard him sliding to a new spot.

An eternity passed before her signature color flared. She sensed all the eyes that spotted her from the abyss.

Am I next?

When the deep shadows returned, she slunk to the side a few meters. There would be no rest tonight.

Now what?

18

AFTERSHOCKS

A RARE SILENCE FELL on the OBD Production Studio. Sudhira anticipated Deandra's next directions as she stared at the screens, cameras zooming into frightened faces for ratings while she, too, realized along with millions of viewers that they had been watching a simulation all along.

What has the world come to when you can't expect your reality entertainment to be real?

Pham wound up and swung a right hook, connecting with the cheekbone of the man strapped to a chair. That collaborator recovered from the blow, spit blood at his feet, and mumbled curses through his swollen jaw, but no secrets.

A phone buzzed from the table in the darkened room, windows covered with posters, tape, and thick shades. The text from Sarge read, "Charlotte OBD, last ten minutes. Major reveal."

He wiped his hand with a bloody rag, slid his laptop around and navigated to that stream, assessing the unfolding replay with dispassionate calculations to the soundtrack of background moans. He texted back. "Explains why Ho Chi Minh OBD had no furniture the next day. I'll bet you'll find a metal band around the walls, and those are the transmitters."

After tossing down the phone and tossing back another gulp of his Singha, he returned to his task.

"My associate just shared a secret about your masters, but that does not get you off the hook. You still owe me your secrets before we're done."

Rafiq danced in a circle with his five-year-old daughter, Shada. She giggled, laughed, and kicked her feet to her own beat. His chant supplied the lyrics.

"Daddy was right. Daddy was right."

"What were you right about, Daddy?" She clapped hands above her head, twisting sock-covered feet back and forth along the bare floor.

"What was I right about? Uh, the thing, the data stream to, uh, a place."

"What's a data stream, Daddy?" Hands on hips bent them left and right.

"What's a data stream? Well, uh, it's data, uh, streaming, like ... a stream."

"What's data, Daddy?" Twirls and twirls flinging curls and curls.

"Data is, uh. You know what, my little Pelican. It doesn't matter. Let's just be happy for Daddy and dance, okay?"

"Deal, Daddy."

19

Math and Sport, Not Tribalism

Tula, Zimbabwean survivor of a Chinese slaughter in the Vietnamese hellhole, panted while pacing the small, strange bedroom practicing his lines. Scratch paper scattered on the desk recorded a teenager's math formulas with plenty of eraser marks and cross-outs. Yeah, he had struggled with trig, too. A medal from a local soccer tournament hung with care on the friend-of-a-friend-of-a-friend's wall. These reminded him of what he fought for.

Home now after days bouncing on both seas and roads, he hated that resolve would not release him from his promise, trapped by conviction. Cramped quarters on the cargo ship provided plenty of time to reflect, and busses crammed with travelers of various backgrounds confirmed his conclusions. Though all looked different on the outside, though all started and ended journeys in various places, they all shared this leg, and at least for this one stretch they lived, laughed, and swapped stories and fruit in peace while bumping shoulders and smelling each other's sweat.

The consequences of his once-in-a-lifetime trigger pull cursed him for eternity. However, a fervor to convert that hex into a blessing burned in his heart. *Turn all things for the good.* The moment he stepped foot in his country, he tracked down the local resistance. It wasn't dying that scared him now; it was living as if already dead—that, and public speaking.

A knock on the door inflated his fear. "Cameras on. Soundcheck good. Stream is up and stable. Ready when you are, Tula."

Today's speaker wiped palms across jeans. Fringe channels from around the globe advocating for a general human uprising distributed this live speech, desperate to spark a fire of rebellion. It didn't matter if one watched or a million; anxiety suffocated the same. His vision narrowed as he pushed lead feet out the door and into the living room turned makeshift studio, ending at the couch in front of a hand-painted resistance banner. The teleprompter scrolling his speech dominated his vision.

"Hello. My name is Tula Moyo from Zimbabwe. If your home is Earth, please listen. If you are not from this planet, listen anyway, because your brief reign of oppression will soon end. You will recognize me from the Ho Chi Minh City One-Bullet Dilemma room where I," he gulped, "*caused* untold thousands of human deaths, all unjustified. For that, I publicly and solemnly apologize. To this day, I lie awake wondering how I could have solved that problem peacefully, without bloodshed, but I fail every night. So, I fight."

He blinked, reached for the nearby glass of water, and guzzled half. Saying it out loud in practice did not thump his chest like speaking it live to the world. Now everyone knew which side he chose.

"When I crawled out of that hellhole, I was thrilled to be alive, but also disgusted. Why did I survive? Why did Benjiro and Gang, and all they represent, have to die? Benjiro was kind, and he calmed me when I was scared. Why did Gang hate so much that he believed the aliens and sacrificed himself just to kill others? How does anyone know that after we entertain them, they won't turn and wipe us all out? What good is our hatred when we are all dead?

"So, I fight, for Benjiro and Gang, for their memory, for their impossible dilemma. I fight, so our children do not have to face such horror."

He found his eyes drifting downward and his mind wandering back to that bedroom. He snapped those eyes back to the red light on the camera and improvised his next line. "Children should focus on math and sport, not tribalism. That is the better future." Then he returned to the prepared text.

"When I climbed that ladder, opened the hatch to the warm sunshine on my face, I yearned to emerge into my old life, go back to my family and friends. Instead, my nightmare continued. Rather than the comfort of home, a strange country, foreign language, and angry stares haunted me on every street. Surely, the families of all those the occupiers snatched from homes and executed would hunt me down and exact revenge, and who could blame them? I did not want Benjiro and Gang to die, but I longed to live. With so much division sewn between us, why would these hurt and grieving people help a stranger, help the stranger who signed their death warrants?"

He grinned.

"But strangers did help. The Ho Chi Minh City resistance found me first, before an angry husband, or brother, or son. I don't even know their names. They found me and brought me home, back to my family and friends. The Vietnamese did not have to help a Zimbabwean, but they did, because no matter the nation, no matter the religion, no matter the health index, we are all human. If a tan-skinned man helped me," he lifted his black arm to the camera, "then surely I can help a white-skinned one, and the white man can help the brown. Together, we help each other.

"So, now, I fight. I fight to heal the hurts between us, to remind us who we all are, that we are all the same inside. I fight to unite us against our oppressor. I fight to remind us how much we share in common."

He paused, leaned into the camera, and concluded, "So, will you fight?"

After an eternity, the show producer ended Tula's torture. "And we're off. Excellent speech, Tula. So genuine. The people will love you. Now, let's get you to safety in the tunnels until we schedule follow-up interviews. You just launched a revolution. How does it feel?"

20

THE OFFER

G REEN COULDN'T SLEEP THAT night, nor could he stay awake. Eyes collapsed under the weight of drowsiness, but on-again-off-again lights jolted them back open a slit.

The final unsealing, though, progressed gently. The torture must have ended, and he must have slept soundly because his rested body eased into the new day. Soft rays slowly brightened as he rose from the hard ground. Rock walls replaced iron bars. His gun nestled snugly under his belt. No enemies lurked.

As he knocked along those new walls listening for a gap and planning his revenge, seething at Blue's betrayal, an opening appeared, stone shifting apart with a deep scraping. A contraption emerged, some kind of self-propelled dolly transporting a man, standing, outstretched arms strapped to a beam in the shape of a cross. His robe draped to above the ankles, bare feet likewise bound. He sported a full, untrimmed beard, and no Agal held his headscarf in place. This was a pious man. His voice, however, sounded hideous, soulless and hollowed like an agonized ghost.

"Come close, Rasheed, and I will guide you to the correct path."

Agitated that this stranger knew his name and suspecting a trap, Green drew his pistol and circled the spectacle from a distance before approaching.

"Do you remember this vessel, Rasheed?"

Blood red filled the man's unblinking eyes—no white sclera, no brown iris, no black pupil. His wrinkled face never flinched. It just stared upward. The voice emerged fully formed from somewhere around the man's head, crystal clear but a notch louder than normal. Something shifted in his beard.

Green stepped back. "Imam?" It had been, what, ten years since he'd kneeled in that Iranian mosque, choosing instead to occasionally put in his time at one in whatever city he happened to visit for business. The hometown adherents were too strident, too rigid for his tastes.

"Yes. I present an offer from our judges."

"What did they do to you? Are you ... dead? Drugged?"

"No. I am connected temporarily. I volunteered my body so they can communicate to you directly with no misinterpretation. The world believes they are conquerors from another planet, but you and I know better, don't we? Nothing happens that was not meant to be."

"Yes, Imam. Our duty is to live rightly until the end. What is the offer?" He thought the Imam—or his 'judges'—tested him like when he was a teenager. *Just get to the point.*

"You have struggled to defeat both rivals and protect your people, like we have always struggled. This was the righteous path, but it is impossible. There is no way to win—no human way, that is—but now your perseverance is rewarded. I offer you a path to defeat both."

Finally, he stood on the verge of a breakthrough, the edge he needed to win this contest, return to his life, not to mention watch both Blue and Red die.

Toughest choice was deciding which should go first. His swelling pride pumped a little more blood through his heart. For weeks he had suffered the weight of responsibility, and now his suffering ended in victory. Lifting that weight released boiling emotions, which pushed tears into each eye.

"What is it? A second bullet? Another weapon? Poison? Guide me on the correct path."

"You must kill yourself."

Martyrdom! His chest pounded; lungs struggled to inhale enough oxygen to survive; his mind blanked. How does that anachronism win?

"No. No way. I am not strapping a bomb to my chest. What kind of cliche do you think I am?" Green shuffled backward until he ran out of floor.

"No need for a bomb when you have a bullet."

Green stared at the gun, struggling to think. Living in the modern, western world most of his adult life enlightened his perspective. Though he loved his people, their history, their strength, their morality, and fought for their advancement, he understood them in a broader context. They were human, too, subject to common, selfish failings. Despite the different cultures, he stood amazed at the familiar threads that wove them together.

For example, pawns from all around the world always sacrificed more on the battlefield than kings, and he was no pawn. He ruled his own life and nobody would manipulate him. Rushing to the dolly, he pressed the end of the barrel against the Imam's forehead.

"Maybe I shoot you, instead, and walk out that hallway you opened up."

No response. Nothing twitched. Nothing.

Green pressed the gun harder. "You're in this room now. Does that make you a player like me? Maybe your death counts, satisfies the requirements, gets me off the hook."

Nothing.

"Argh!" Green re-tucked his gun and stomped away.

"Rasheed, remember how powerless you were in your vision? How passive? You had no choice but to swim along the torrent of fate. Now, however …"

He rubbed his arm, phantom burn still stinging.

"Remember how your people suffered. Remember how we are corrupted today. You know all too well since you live among the corrupters. This is how you serve your people."

"I'm not a martyr. I serve my people with my life, improve my people's lives with my own."

"Of course, and get rich along the way. Don't think of it as martyrdom, Rasheed. Think of it as a tactic that puts power in your hands. You will control destiny. You will win, decisively, like you've always wanted to win since you were a young boy."

Green strode the outer wall, pounding the stone. When he reached the Imam's entrance, he stared down an unlit tunnel. No new clues to where he was or what lay beyond his prison. No clue if he could run and escape, but it may have been worth a try. If he died, at least he'd die on his terms, fighting.

Grr. The world would just see me die while running away.

"There is only one way out." His former Imam laid out the terms of the deal. "You will pass away and go to your reward. Our predetermined demographic also perishes, but I have assurance that all of them will be weak. Can't have our judges viewed as not keeping their word. In return, a portion of your opponents' people also die. Combined, it amounts to more than if you only defeated one. What happens after is a bonus, and our people will count them as your slain, too. That means more kafir killed in a single day than all our victories in history combined, Rasheed. Your name will be immortal."

He soaked in the proposal, mind churning through the options. One business lesson he never forgot was that golden opportunities were rare. Grind the day-to-day and progress slowly, or risk it all for the big win. Take the simple out, kill Blue for revenge and let Red have her way, or take the bullet and die knowing he went out on top.

The self-driving dolly retreated, eventually enveloped by murkiness in the tunnel, the Imam's eerie voice reaching out one last time before the new entrance closed shut with a solid thud.

"Remember your people. Remember your brothers. We will remember this day."

Red wept, a continual, un-pluggable drip that soaked both sleeves, front collar, and the body of her shirt. Every justification Blue offered pumped the well a little more.

"Green was a wildcard. You know that. You saw for yourself. He aimed his gun at you first. I may have saved your life."

Her gun was already jammed into her blue jeans' waistband. Vision blurred, mind blank except for streaks of incoherent images, the timeline from recent days jumbled into ever-evolving narratives: Mark as reliable partner, Blue as calculating competitor. She was in no condition to defend herself and, honestly, didn't particularly care at that moment whether she lived or died. The muscles in her gut cramped from all the spasms. *You used to make me smile. Why would you turn on me like this?*

"You know I tried to get us all out. Man, I tried. I've never desired anything more in my life than to see you and me climb out of here together, but it seemed clear he'd snap at any moment. Removing him lets you and me work it out."

She bolted along the back wall toward Green's room, anywhere to escape the logic backstabbing her emotions, but Blue shadowed along the porous inner cell buffer that failed to block his voice. The barrier between her and the silent one, however, comprised solid rock. She pounded on it. *Damn it, Green.* What else was there to simulate? This was the endgame, decision time, time to smash all hope of surviving together—*time to accept I'm going to die, alone, or live with your death on my conscience forever.*

"There's still hope for us, Willa. Remember I told you all my plans were crazy? I still have one for us, if you want to hear it."

She sprang halfway to him, anguished. "I trusted you. You nursed me when I was sick. I felt safe around you, and now this?" He had said he wanted to work with her, then stabbed Green in the side. Would he stab her in the back next? He had said cooperation would free them, then he went rogue.

Fleeing the empty promises to the other empty corner, as far from both male disappointments as possible, she faced the soulless stone, palms smacking all along searching for an escape.

"I want you as my partner, Willa."

She stopped slapping the wall, tears subsiding. Palms and forehead leaned against it while the final drips of snot fell from the tip of her nose. The numbing slab soaked the last heat of her ire.

"Green refused to join the struggle. I simplified the situation. I was thinking about us."

She rolled her back along the wall to face her tormentor, tired eyes awakening to the fact she needed to form some kind of reply, to process his claims and either accept or deny them.

She murmured, "You liked my story without knowing it was mine."

"What was that?"

Heavy eyes fell away from his puppy face. "Nothing." It didn't matter, anyway. Their entire room, their current world, had faded before their eyes. If this was the end, she wanted to at least hold on to the illusion of validation.

She forced herself to move. Weighty steps paced the periphery toward Green's room, eyes to the floor, both hands stuck to a forehead holding back her scalp, deliberating. Metal greeted her at the end, not a boulder.

She looked up and found Green, standing in the center of his room as calm as any professor on a normal day at school, gun pointed triumphantly to the sky. She fumbled to draw hers.

"Don't bother, Red. I finally defeated you both. Told you I would."

With that epitaph, Green placed the muzzle to his temple and fired his one bullet, resignation chiseled on his face. The blast formed the baseline to the treble of her continual screech, harmonizing with the receding echoes throughout the chamber, coalescing into a chorus of horror.

The slightly metallic odor of blood had unpacked its bags and moved in. Green's body lay serenely on the bare ground, crimson puddle spreading from under his head, and Red suffered a kindred spirit inside: lifeless. She didn't love the man—didn't hate him either—and disdained his worldview. But through numerous conversations—heated yet forthright—at least understood his motivations. She never wanted him dead, just gone so she could live her best life.

The circular fence surrounding the escape ladder had already turned. Only one layer stood between her and freedom. Still impenetrable, though.

She sat deflated, back against the outer wall. Her one remaining frenemy glued himself to the rods separating him and Green, speechless for the first time since they'd arrived.

For hours, his hands gripped the bars, face pushed through to the other side. His longest motion entailed sliding down the smooth metal once knees buckled.

"Mark?" Her call separated his head from its vice.

He turned and forced a fleeting smile. "Hey." With a sigh, he rolled his back against Green's bars, gun settled between bent knees. "Guess it's just us now."

Joyless voice and empty affect: Green's action traumatized them both. They had shared laughs, talks, and arguments, now they partook in pain. A small, instinctual part of her that wanted to comfort him knew no words. The bulk of her soul still feared him, though.

After several more minutes of silence, he cleared his throat. "Remember way back on day one when we figured out whoever shoots first loses? Well, the game has changed. Now, whoever shoots first wins."

What a weird thought. This entire time, she presumed he mourned. Instead, he schemed. The implications of their tactical position never crossed her mind. Her concern focused on people, on how this touched her. What if she ever found herself cornered by Green's family? How would she explain this? No hug would suffice. Blue's logic rang true, yet why would he say that?

Spirit of the wolf. She leaped to her feet, gun sprung up, both hands gripping that protector, sights steady on the menace, ready to pull that trigger first. Heart thumped with a purpose. Eyes narrowed on the threat.

He did not escalate. Instead, he slowly rose to his feet, holstered his firearm, and sauntered to the center of his room, meters away.

Her barrel followed.

"Want to hear my ultimate grand plan? Spoiler alert—it's crazy," he said.

The final showdown, then. She could end him or listen.

"No sudden moves, Mark. I swear to God I'll shoot!" Dad had taught her how to defend herself, how to survive teenager years as a female in a rough neighborhood. She would not let him down now that she had come so far, achieved so many of his dreams.

He raised hands in surrender. "Hear me out first, okay? Then decide." She nodded consent. "This entire situation is FUBAR; we all agreed about that. We're thrown into a humanly impossible position by psychos and told to dance for their entertainment, but what if we flipped the script? What if we produced our own game, wrote our own rules?"

She remembered this was the guy who sharpened a lamp's bulb socket into a shiv and tried to electrocute another human being. He always had a plan.

"What are my options, really?" Blue continued the reveal. "If you died, the world loses something special, something precious. That's terrible, don't you think?"

He prowled one step.

"What are you up to, Mark?" She did not drop her guard, every blink purposefully brief in order to maintain the vigil.

"But worse than that, if you died … I'd have to live the rest of my life without you, and I realized that would be a constant death inside of me. So, lose-lose."

Her muzzle dipped just a bit. It had been many moons since someone hinted they wanted her around.

"I'm going to draw my weapon, slowly, I promise."

The safety gap between them narrowed another stride.

She flinched, deadly aim returned to target, peripheral tuned to any sudden movements.

He just spoke slowly. "You are smart …"

That sounded like a generic compliment meant to disarm her, like a marketer's opening line before his sales pitch. Slow as a sloth, he removed his gun from his waistband with one hand and raised it high, business end pointed safely away from her.

He inched ahead.

"Sarcastic …"

True, personalized at least, and sounded sincere. Gravity dropped the magazine into his waiting other hand.

What is he up to?

Gingerly, he stooped and slid the pistol underneath her bars to between her feet. He crept ever closer.

She trotted away from the gift; maybe it was a bomb. Her head rotated left and right, sweeping the entire chamber for threats.

"Drop dead gorgeous …"

Whatever.

His face was candid, or naive. His words guileless. They eased her tension, but adrenaline kept her focused. She enjoyed the moment, and hated it, wanted to run to the safety of a comfortable bed, tumble under the sheets and think.

Hands still in plain view, he removed his one bullet from the top of the stack and tossed the magazine through the billets, clanging on the other side of her room. This was sadistic. Make your move already and get it over with.

"Think about it. We're great together. We survived this horror show so far. What else in life would ever separate us?"

"What are you saying?" A watery blur clouded her vision; dry throat constricted.

He encroached two more deliberate steps.

Like a jab to elicit a block and open up a hole in his defenses, she dashed to the buffer between them, gun still on her side of the bars, safe from his snatch, free to counter any attack, barrel wavering a little.

He clenched his eyes for a few seconds, then opened them and sighed in relief. The stoic metal hedge halted his advance mere centimeters away. She could either pistol-whip him or hug him through the bars. Hands made no sudden gestures except for a visible shake. He kneeled on one trembling knee.

Her muzzle lowered to follow, pressed against his forehead.

She commanded complete control. "Why shouldn't I just end you now and climb up that dumb ladder?"

"Because I practiced this speech for days, so ... please don't?"

Nervous and fumbling, he set his one bullet on the horizontal crossbar. It plinked to the floor. One hand kept the surrender posture while the other retrieved the tiny, valuable peace offering, and this time successfully presented it before her.

"It's not a diamond, but it is forged from a stone all the same." Blue cracked a tiny smile and shrugged quaking shoulders.

She swayed, weight shifting from foot to frightened foot.

"Willa ... I love you."

Like his out-loud profession, more tears surprised her. Stunned, she dropped her gun to her side and brought a free hand to her gaping mouth. "Are you being serious right now?"

"Life without you is meaningless. End this nightmare and marry me?"

She sniffled, deeply, and joined him on her knees. "Mark, if you are punking me, please stop and just kill me right now. I can't take this."

"No cap, Willa. As far as I'm concerned, you should either say 'yes' or kill me right now. There's no point in winning if it means I lose you. No matter what happens, nobody who leaves will really be alive, will they?"

She set down her gun and extended gentle hands through the iron blooms, cupping his quivering face. Then she reached one hand back and slid the gun a little further away from his grasp. "I'm not saying no, but how does this help us get out of here?"

"It may not. It may mean lights-out for both of us. Who knows, but I'd rather live a few minutes with your love than an entire lifetime with just your memory."

Oh wow, his eyes were brown. They were either the best liars she had ever seen or they gazed on her with genuine affection, wholesome and tender.

Now what?

21

Coupon. Text. Pill. 9-1-1

"T HIS IS THE BEST chance we'll ever get. Blue made the bold move, and the people love it. We use that momentum, take the station, broadcast our recruitment pitch. It either works, or I die in the counterattack. It's okay to be scared, Noor, but if you're in, recap the plan once more."

Sudhira detected Sarge's heightened tension over the phone. He was always serious in his mission, but charming in his interactions. She missed that smile she had never seen except in her mind, but knew this moment needed focus, not flattery. Her choice was simple. Take an active role in coworkers dying, or back out and watch millions more die on her planet.

"Coupon. Text. Pill. 9-1-1. Wait for you to bring me flowers, preferably lotus." She cracked her own nervous smile, the kind that pretends the previous words were half-jokes and that hopes the reply is all serious.

"You do your best, stay safe above all else, and I'll do my best. Sarge out."

That sounded sincere, at least, if not curt, as the burner phone disconnected, leaving Sudhira to her narrowing thoughts.

"Time to earn your codename, Noor. Let's write a better ending this time, shall we?"

Coupon

The hood ripped off Sudhira's head rougher than normal that day. The van's side door slammed open. Eyes of building security stared as she stepped into the garage and toward the metal detectors. All followed her every move—no one else; just her—but none stopped her.

A guard carried the metal lockbox trapping all the worker's phones into the small office. They confiscated them when each worker first stepped into the van. So, if Sarge needed it to ping a tower so he could narrow down the studio's location to a five-block area, Sudhira prayed one of the guards loved biryani.

Before entering the elevator, she broke from the pack, shuffled to the security desk, and forced a smile. "I am so sorry to bother you." Stiff hands circled and shuffled as if they could distract the burly guy from her shaky voice. "My cousin just opened her dream restaurant downtown. Best Indian Fusion you'll ever eat, I promise. I brought coupons for free meals but forgot them in my cellphone case. It's the flower print one. Grab them and pass them around. It'll really help my cousin. Thanks."

She quick-stepped to catch up with the crew filing into the elevator. As the doors slid shut, she threw out one more pitch.

"Free food tastes better."

After the elevator doors closed, the guard behind the desk peered around. No other coworkers stood nearby, so he unlocked the phone box, fumbled around for the flower print case, and found several coupons slipped into the back pouch. He flipped one around, eyed the featured dishes, and pocketed all of them.

Sarge lay on his couch, one leg flopped over the side, hand holding the television remote switching between his local OBD and a nature show on stealth predators. A relaxing Saturday mid-morning if he hadn't been so eager for news about Noor. As such, the tense day dragged along like solo guard duty.

His phone buzzed. The text from Five-by-Five read, "Found your friend. Map pin on its way to Sierra squad."

He replied, "Nice. Once Sierra arrives, send the text." At least Deandra would enjoy her morning.

Time for these stealth predators to tighten the noose around their prey.

Sarge turned off the television, rolled off his couch, and slid it forward. Prying up a group of floorboards unveiled his stash of firearms. He lifted Paco, as in Paco Sanchez, as in an FN PS90, his absolute favorite close quarters battle rifle. Long time, old friend. *Wish it were just another weekend on the range.*

He sent another text. "Alpha, come gear up. Time to hunt."

Text

Deandra zoned out, mentally rose to another plane—the highest, most productive one possible. Headaches, stomach grumbles, coworker complaints, all faded while she focused on those ratings. Zoned up was more like it.

"Clark, jot the phrase 'Zoned Up.' Read it back to me later," she blurted to her assistant then returned to rocking her job of directing the live OBD feed.

Blue's proposal shocked the scripted reality industry. No one saw it coming, and the Network ordered she milk it for every eyeball possible.

Her phone buzzed. A text. She read it twice before fist-pumping the air and shouting out a hallelujah.

"Everyone, listen. Just got a heads-up from the Network. The Academy nominated us for an Emmy!"

Cheers rose from everyone, stuffing the production studio with even more energy. Everyone, except one. Sudhira's arms did not join the rest in the air, but still locked to the camera joysticks, eyes frozen forward, right leg jittering.

"You okay?" Deandra laid a hand on Sudhira's trembling shoulder.

She turned up her face, tense, Indian tan skin paled a few shades of yellow.

"You look ill, girl," Deandra said.

Sudhira cracked a fake smile. "Yeah, I'm okay. No ... no, not really. I need to step away for a minute."

"Yeah, go take your break. Sam will cover for a few. You need some pills? Cause I got pills."

"No, no. Thanks." Sudhira rose from her seat, dead-eyed, and shuffled out the studio door toward the restroom.

Pill

Sudhira, alone in the bathroom, stared down at the pills in her hand, up at the stranger in the mirror, and back at the pills. The drugs were risky. The plan was risky.

Thinking about it too much was risky, so she slammed them back and swallowed hard.

After chugging her bottled water, silent eyes found a familiar face smiling from the mirror. "You are Noor Inayat-Khan. You will save your people."

She stumbled out of the bathroom into the hallway.

9-1-1

Deandra loved her morning, but sensed a headache flaring up even before the interruption.

Teddy burst through the door to the production studio, slamming it wide open. "Help! Sudhira passed out in the hallway. Deandra, call 9-1-1."

Deandra churned and yelled an obscenity before his words sunk in. Her anger then ebbed into concern for Sudhira.

Teddy stood, whitened face, mouth agape, hand reaching for her lifeline to the Network. Concern flowed into fear of missing a message from her boss at this critical moment in the show.

She hesitated.

"Come on, Deandra. You have the only phone on the floor."

Eyes flitted between Teddy and her phone until her crystal-clear vision returned. She shot out her hand for him to take it. Fear of failure spiraled into self-loathing for pausing way too long to help Sudhira. To cope, she downed a Xanax and refocused on the myriad of screens plastering the wall in front of her. The show must go on.

Sierra squad, scouts of the resistance, arrived at the map location Five-by-Five sent them. Three cars, one member each, fanned out to park two blocks away … and waited.

Ate chips, and waited.

Played music, and waited.

Squinted in the noon sun, and waited.

Finally, a siren stirred Sierra Two's senses. An ambulance screamed past. He texted the rest of the squad and pursued until it stopped at a three-story building. Flashing lights bounced off the brick and glass walls.

He joined the gathering onlookers and waited until a gurney exited the building. Snapping a pic with his phone and zooming in on the patient's face, he compared it to the dating profile Sarge provided. It matched as best as he could tell with an oxygen mask added in real life.

Noor lay on top, strapped down, unconscious.

Jittery fingers hammered out his next text.

"Bingo."

Sarge screeched his brakes and angled his car across the sidewalk to one side of the front door. A second car from Alpha squad matched him on the other side, the two forming a 'V' pointing away from the building, barricading the entrance and offering cover. The rest of Alpha and Bravo squads converged in an instant. Charlie breached the rear of the building. Sierra maintained a stealth perimeter to observe and report. Five-by-Five hunkered down in his undisclosed communications bunker.

Fifteen shooters, three spotters, and a brave spy who pinpointed the enemy's location. Time to launch a revolution. Time to go all in and see who wins.

Sarge's mind and body were both numb to the periphery and hyper-sensitive to the moment. Focused. He seemed to watch the unfolding scene as if detached from the first-person perspective while still maintaining full control. The front door's outline, his next waypoint, almost glowed.

Armed and masked, he burst out of his car, pointed two shooters to the redoubt, and sprinted into the building, Paco Sanchez—his trusty PS90—shouldered and pointed ahead.

Two lobby security guards standing in front of their desk gawked as he glided toward them. One hand moved to a holster.

"Don't do it!" Sarge warned.

He did.

Bang, bang. Sarge won the death race and planted two rounds center mass, blasting that guard against the desk. Deal with those emotions later.

The second guard froze, face whiter than a hospital wall, hands smartly held out in submission.

"Where's the production studio?" Sarge demanded, Paco Sanchez translating his intent in case it wasn't clear.

An arm lifted as if pressing a record-breaking weight, finger pointing up. "Which floor?"

Three stiff fingers shook in the breezeless air. Sporadic shots and escalating screams resounded from the rest of the ground floor. Sarge's earpiece crackled.

"Alpha One, this is Charlie One. Guessing target is on third floor since the elevator won't go without a badge."

"Alpha One, copy. Meet you there."

He pointed Paco Sanchez away from the shaking guard and gently reached for the badge dangling from his belt. "I'll take that. Now move to the elevator."

He pressed his radio's talk button. "Bravo, grab badges and cover the stairwells. Breach on my mark."

Sarge and five shooters, along with two security personnel—now hostages—met inside the ground floor elevator. He positioned the security team in front as shields and waited for Bravo.

"Bravo in position."

He swiped the badge and hit the third-floor button. His ears filtered out everything except that *ding*. "Breach! Breach!"

Elevator doors glided open to a peaceful scene. Empty hallways. No guards. No shootouts. Bravo One turned a corner, signaling an 'all clear.' Bravo Two appeared at the other end of the hallway, pushing two hostages in front.

Too quiet for his tastes. He sensed a trap.

"Which room?" Sarge tapped the lobby guard's shoulder, who pointed straight ahead. "Go." Sarge shoved him onward.

The troops crept to the room and lined the hostages against the wall. Sarge and another burst open the door. A room full of clueless faces took several seconds to notice and one-by-one look away from their screens.

He hurried along the attention-gathering phase. "Who used to be in charge here? Because make no mistake about it, that job is now mine."

He followed the lines of multiple faces from across the room as they turned, triangulating on the only woman who hadn't yet noticed him. She stood staring at the wall of screens, arms crossed holding a tablet to her chest, phone jittering in a hand, foot tapping an unheard beat.

Deandra. She looked as energetic and itchy as Noor had described.

She barked out an order, and, when nobody reacted, she whipped around to yell a follow-up. He smiled at her shocked face.

"What's your name, boss lady?" Playing ignorant lowered the risk of burning Noor as his mole.

"Deandra, and who are you? We didn't request more security."

"Don't worry, Deandra. We won't hit your budget, but I need a favor."

She flashed him a look that warned he should be careful with his next words. There were some requests she would not tolerate.

"I need you to put a camera on me and jack me into the One-Bullet Dilemma feed."

Rafiq slurped chickpea soup in between matches of hand-slap with Shada. She giggled every time he let her win, which means he won the greater prize.

A laptop on the table, screen turned away from her and volume turned off, streamed the Charlotte OBD room. The screen blackened, replaced seconds later with a masked man, view from his waist up. A rifle hung in front. An address in bold text, all caps, scrolled across the bottom third.

"Ooo, honey, Daddy's got to listen to this. Go play in your room, okay?"

He turned up the volume.

"Civilians of Charlotte, friends, humans. This is not a commercial. We are live for a brief interruption. My name is Sarge, and I have seized control of the One-Bullet Dilemma production studio."

Sarge looked off screen as someone handed him a tablet. He read it, nodded, handed it back, then returned his focus to the camera.

"I'll be quick because my time is short, unless you help. The cops and national guard will arrive in force soon, I'm sure, to capture or kill us, all on the orders of those aliens floating in the skies above. This OBD is their number one weapon against Earth, and we intend to end it.

"My pitch is simple. You know in your heart that what they are doing to split us up, herd us up, and kill us is wrong. I need you. Come now to the address on your screen and help us hold this position. We plan to find that OBD and rescue Red and Blue ..."

He hung his head.

"Sorry. How easy is it to become dehumanized by constant propaganda? We will rescue *Willa* and *Mark*, people, not colors, not labels, from that hellhole.

"Do not wait. Do not hesitate. You've had plenty of time to think it over. You know you've been chomping at the bit for a chance to fight back, and this is it. If you do not rise up now, our region is lost."

Sarge gestured for the camera to zoom in on him. Masked face filled the screen—honest, bloodshot eyes in high-resolution staring at the audience.

"Please. Come. Everybody. No special skills needed. We have a plan to organize you and put you into action right away. You are the resistance."

With that closing plea, Sarge left the frame. Moments later the live OBD feed returned, address still stuck in the chyron.

Rafiq gulped his remaining dinner and slung gear over his shoulder. His wife eyed his every move. She knew. He strode to her and wrapped her in a gentle hug. "This is the call. I must go."

"I have to ask one last time. Are you certain?"

"No, but fate will decide if we live or die, not an oppressor."

Her eyes worried, but also understood. She let his hug slip away.

He swung by his daughter's room on the way out. "Come here, Shada, my little pelican. Give daddy a big hug. I have to go make the world better for you, okay? I may be late. Don't wait up. Say your prayers, do your homework, so I can check it when I return. Daddy loves you."

Sudhira stared at a blah ceiling, burning coursing through her veins—tolerable but keeping her from sleep. The nurse said the sensation would subside in a few hours after the chemical flush pumped out any remaining toxins. Apparently, two days was not enough suffering.

Stories of the exploding resistance movement and sporadic counterattacks by disorganized National Guard units dominated the news. OBD ratings plummeted. Maybe nobody cared about watching different tribes cooperate and even like each other. Deandra texted numerous times, assuring her their team's Emmy would still be awarded.

A gentle rap sounded from her door. A tall, black man dressed in a US Space Force uniform stood in the entrance holding a beautiful purple and pink bouquet.

"Do you know how hard lotus flowers are to find in this town?" he quipped.

His smile shined exactly the way she envisioned from their many phone calls.

22

POSTER COUPLE

*M*ARRIED LIFE WASN'T SO *hard*. Mark grinned.

At least not compared to filing through a metal bar with nothing but cotton threads, chips of stones, plus sharpened buttons and zippers from his pants. He and Willa sat and worked on the same beam surrounding the ladder, though from different sides. The idea: expose enough of a gap for her to squeeze her skinny self through and climb to find a rescue party.

"We're making good progress today." Willa's eyes twinkled as she sawed, and that satisfied him.

He could not see her smile through the makeshift bandana she wore smothered in whatever sauce and seasoning that came with their meals—anything to filter the stench from Rasheed's rotting corpse a few meters away—but she was more animated, more invested in her escape, in their future, than he had seen since the early, dank days.

"Yeah. At this pace we'll finish a day or so before I turn completely insane," he replied. "Oh, wait, there go those noises again, crystal clinking at our wedding reception, I swear. Our five-hundred guests demand me to kiss you once more."

He held onto the plan, the dream, needed the allure of a happy ending to keep his mind treading the waters of despair.

The couple gulped less putrid air, raised their marinated masks, and lingered on a loving smooch through the bars until one of their exhausted lungs deflated.

"Mmm. That never gets old." It was his turn to smile and take over the cutting duties.

She stood and shook out her legs. "I haven't agreed to wedding plans yet, or to a wedding."

He looked up and smiled, still swiping that six-inch long, twisted cotton saw back and forth around an imperceptible groove in the unyielding iron. "I know, but a boy can dream." He had crafted his plan, made his choice. If death came, it would find him pursuing love, not hate. Besides, this was the most content his spirit had been in years.

"So, what kind of couple are we? Are we like a trauma couple connected only by a crappy situation? As long as we perpetually stay in tragedy mode, we'll be fine? Will we stare at each other one day and realize we have nothing in common?" Willa crossed her arms and nibbled on a thumbnail.

"Better a trauma couple than a drama couple."

She paused her nibbling. "Well, yeah. That goes without saying. Nobody *wants* drama."

"I know, right? But seriously, this dilemma is not who we are. It just made us stronger, more sure of each other. The more I learned about you these past weeks, the more there was to love."

"What if we escape? How do you know how you'll feel when life returns to normal?"

He smiled at her and sawed a little more vigorously. "Escape or not, you are my new normal. I'm committed to you. I'll be by your side if you want me."

"What if we can't get out? What if no one rescues us?"

He detected her breath quickening. That thought haunted his dreams as well, but he would not give in. "Then I hope they find our skeletons laying on the ground cuddling through these bars."

"Huh. Morbid, and sweet. How do you pull off being weird so well?"

He shrugged his shoulders. "No clue. Guess it's a gift."

"What if we escape and have no more chaos? What if you look at me one day and think to yourself, 'I don't want to kill her anymore, so now I want to kill myself to be rid of this boredom?'" She finger-gunned her brain.

The reminder that he had, in fact, attempted to murder someone stabbed his gut. His arm twitched at a phantom pain in his rib. He clammed up, focused on blowing grit away from that metal to sail the horror out of his mind. It didn't drift away so easily.

"Mark? You still with me?"

"I never wanted to kill anyone." He couldn't look up at her. His chest tightened, heart thumped a guilty beat, and eyesight blurred.

Her tone softened. "I know. I meant metaphorically, of course. Sorry." She sat, reached her hand through the bars, and placed a gentle hand on his shoulder.

Minutes passed before he mustered the courage to speak without crying. "At least the food keeps coming. Thank God for that."

"Can't enjoy gladiators fighting to the death while they're starving."

"Or maybe the aliens have a bureaucracy that hasn't noticed the show cancellation. Wouldn't surprise my dad to learn that was a galactic truth."

"Would you ever have guessed that drones flew food down from the ceiling? How did we never figure that out?"

He silently thanked Willa for the mental distraction, something else to discuss besides his moral failings. "Uh, yeah, that." He cleared his throat. "What's your theory? I got nothing."

"Maybe since they completely hijacked our brains ..." She stared into the darkness above and shouted, "Without our consent," before continuing. "It isn't unreasonable that they can remove perception as well as implant it. So, they simply blinded us to the meal until the drone returned to the shadows. Dastardly, really, if you think about it."

Clunk. Thud. Thud.

The newlyweds recoiled from sudden, unfamiliar sounds. He stared at his bride—*fiancé, maybe? What relationship status are we at this point? And what did she trigger?* Her eyes asked the same question. Dust and small stones rained down from the black hole capping their cavern.

"Got it. Over here, got it." A fresh voice boomed from above—a human voice. Flashlight beams penetrated the dark.

Mark and Willa leaped to their feet and trotted along their shared hedge away from the ladder.

Moments later clangs from boots racing down the rungs echoed across the cave, ending with a chunky soldier of some kind emerging from the unlit mystery and sliding the final meters. Dust billowed as feet hit stone. A rifle hung across his back. Nothing in his outfit or gear matched colors or fit well—blue jeans, tattered light sweater, and a baseball cap, all covered with loose straps full of dangling grenades, ammo, and a med kit. But man if he didn't flash a big, beautiful smile when he eyeballed the residents and worked his radio.

"Got em. We got the targets, uh, eyes on targets. Hurrah." Then the soldier gagged. "Oh God, what's that smell?"

They pointed to Rasheed.

"Ugh. Forgot about that." After freeing a bandana from a pocket, he addressed them directly. "Hi, Red. Hi, Blue. It is so good to finally meet you. I'm a huge fan. Come here. Come closer."

The new guy reached into a pouch and extracted what looked like a thick chocolate bar. As they inched forward, though, the delicious treat tempting their taste buds turned into a phone with a camera snapping a pic of three people but only one smile.

The soldier's radio crackled. *"Remember, we're here to rescue them, Rafiq, not get an autograph."*

He blushed and cleared his throat. "I know, er ..." He forgot to press his talk button the first time. "I said I know. Bring the saw." Addressing the captives again, he laid out the situation and answered their questions, gushing the entire time. "My name is Rafiq. I'm a sergeant in the North Carolina Piedmont Militia, 2nd Regiment, 3rd Battalion, but don't quote me on those numbers; they may be backward. We are here to rescue you."

"Are you being serious right now? What's the plan?"

"Well, first we are going to cut these bars so you two can properly hug, and, um ..." he withheld the next piece of information, avoided the punchline. "... you know ..."

"No, we don't know. That's why we asked."

He giggled. "You're going to consummate this marriage on screens across the entire world—LIVE. Think of the ratings." Rafiq smirked and gawked at the celebrities like a blushing creep for way too long before roaring, "Ah, ha-ha. Just kidding. We secured a room for you at a five-star hotel. The fighting blew out one window. We nailed some boards across. It'll be fine."

"And do NOT tell the consummate joke, Rafiq. That's an order."

As the second soldier—this one decidedly more professional—descended and freed the bride and groom, Rafiq filled them in on recent events, yelling over the whine of the circular saw, real flying sparks triggering real traumatizing memories. Mark squeezed Willa's hand through the metal and strained to hear.

"Yeah, the world was ending, you know? We had given up, but when you two fell in love and said 'screw you' to the game plan, no pun intended there, I don't know; it just triggered something subconscious. You know what it was? It reminded us of who we all are, that we are all the same inside. If you two, who from the outside are supposed to be enemies, can come together so intimately, surely we could throw aside our differences to fight genocide. So, we organized better, fought back, you know. We lose a lot, but it's okay because it feels better than giving up. Finding you was top priority from upstairs. You two are now the official poster couple for the resistance. Viva humanity."

The saw dropped a bar from the center circle much faster than braided cotton, getting that tool into her room. Slicing through the top of another iron blockade took forever, but after that, Mark used every opportunity to rage against the weakened bar. The blade overheated; he kicked the bar furiously. The soldier's arm needed rest; Mark pounded, pulled, jiggled, whatever to loosen up that bar. Finally, it fell, and he squeezed between the gap and wrapped two arms around his love, weeping uncontrollably. She rubbed the back of his head, hair flowing over and between her fingers.

She cupped his face. He gazed back through moist eyes.

"You did it, Mark. Freed us both, like you planned from the beginning. You got your way." She paused as her lips quivered. Her whole body trembled against his like subtle rumbles in the ground from a passing train. "Will you change your mind about me?"

Befuddled, he pored over every lovely spot on her face. "Never. I promise. Now, let's go consummate."

That made her smile and blush. Her tense muscles softened and eased further into his chest. Then she punched his arm as they headed for the ladder to rejoin the world.

Love conquers all.

Author Links

Follow Joe on X or visit his website for more info.

https://twitter.com/JoeWriterBenet

http://JoeBenet.com

https://JoeBenet.medium.com/

Enjoy the Story?

Honest reviews help an author more than any marketing campaign. Please rate the book wherever you bought it. It doesn't matter if you found it a mediocre 3-star or a fantastic 5. The number of reviews matters more than the rating. Thank you.